Born and raised on the Wirral Peninsula in England, **Charlotte Hawkes** is mum to two intrepid boys who love her to play building block games with them and who object loudly to the amount of time she spends on the computer. When she isn't writing—or building with blocks—she is company director for a small Anglo/French construction company. Charlotte loves to hear from readers, and you can contact her at her website: charlotte-hawkes.com.

Also by Charlotte Hawkes

The Army Doc's Secret Wife
The Surgeon's Baby Surprise

Hot Army Docs miniseries

Encounter with a Commanding Officer
Tempted by Dr Off-Limits

Discover more at millsandboon.co.uk.

A BRIDE TO REDEEM HIM

CHARLOTTE HAWKES

MILLS & BOON

First published in Great Britain 2018
by Mills & Boon, an imprint of HarperCollins*Publishers*
1 London Bridge Street, London, SE1 9GF

Large Print edition 2018

ISBN: 978-0-263-07310-2

MIX
Paper from
responsible sources
FSC www.fsc.org FSC C007454

This book is produced from independently certified
FSC™ paper to ensure responsible forest management. For
more information visit www.harpercollins.co.uk/green.

Printed and bound in Great Britain
by CPI Group (UK) Ltd, Croydon, CR0 4YY

To Derek,
thanks for reading my books.
Also, for telling people that you do so! x

CHAPTER ONE

SHE WAS STILL SHAKING.

Whether it was through humiliation, anger, or simply an utter sense of failure, Alexandra Vardy—Alex to only her closest friends, Dr Vardy to most of her patients—couldn't be sure.

Whichever it was, it wasn't now helped by the advancing form of infamous surgeon Louis Delaroche, whose smouldering, rebellious, bad-boy self had been plastered over the media for a decade. Between the tabloids, the internet and various entertainment news channels in all manner of graphic shots, the man was the hot topic of conversation at water coolers across the world on practically a weekly basis. And still nothing could have prepared her for the assault on her senses at being alone and this close to him.

Alex gripped the stone balustrade of the ornate external balcony, sucked down lungfuls of the cold night air that penetrated her one and only ballgown, and reminded herself to keep breathing.

In and out. In and out.

'Why were you discussing Rainbow House with my father?' His low voice carried in the darkness.

'Discussing?' She squeezed her eyes closed at the unpleasant memory of the run-in with Jean-Baptiste Delaroche. 'Is that what you call that verbal mauling?'

'Do you want to tell me what happened?'

It wasn't so much a question as a quiet command. Typical Louis. But not sinful playboy Louis; this was all pioneering surgeon Louis. The one gift he gave the world to stop it from burying him completely. She'd seen him in action and his skill was simply breathtaking.

Still, that didn't mean she was about to trust him now. Especially when her thoughts were such a jumbled mess.

'Why would I want to tell you what happened? Aren't *you* supposed to be the mercurial one of the Delaroche Duo, not your father? Isn't he the good one? The one the media hails as one of the true philanthropists of a generation?'

She had truly believed in that image of Jean-Baptiste, had really thought that he would help her once he knew what was planned for Rainbow House. It had never crossed her mind that he might have actually been party to the plans.

To her horror, Alex choked back an unexpected sob. Not with Jean-Baptiste, and not now with Louis. Part of her wanted to flee this balcony, this party, this night. But she couldn't. Not while the fate of Rainbow House still hung in the balance. The centre was the last common ground she and her father shared. If she lost that then she lost him. And they'd both lost so much already.

She might not trust Louis, but she couldn't bring herself not to listen to him.

'That's my father,' Louis concurred tightly. 'Such a good man.'

'You don't agree? Of course you don't.' She threw up her hands in desperation. 'The whole world knows there is bad blood between the two of you. Are you as jealous of your father's good name as they say you are?'

Rather than replying, he lifted his shoulders casually and turned her question back on her. The cool, unflappable, playboy Louis the media loved to hate.

'You still think he deserves his good name? After he just tried to have you thrown out of here?'

Of all the ways he might have spoken to her,

Alex wasn't prepared for the hint of warmth, of kindness.

Almost as if he actually cared.

Her head swam and suddenly it all felt too much.

'I... I don't know.'

Before she could catch herself, she slumped back against the stone balustrade, trying to order the thoughts racing around her head. A fraction of a second later, Louis was shrugging off his tuxedo jacket and settling it gently over her shoulders before resuming his position between her and the doors back inside the estate house. Whether he was protecting her from any security detail should they come looking or blocking her escape, Alex couldn't quite be certain.

The only reason she'd even attended the annual Delaroche Foundation Charity Gala Ball had been in the hope that she would find a quiet moment alone to speak discreetly to the eminent surgeon Jean-Baptiste and ask him if he might possibly reconsider the foundation's unexpected decision to take over and shut down the desperately needed Rainbow House.

She could never have predicted that the media's beloved 'knight in shining scrubs' would turn on her so instantly and with such venom, even going so far as to instruct his security detail to parade her through the ballroom before throwing her out. *To make an example out of her.* Jean-Baptiste's snarl still echoed in her head, causing fresh waves of nausea to swell up inside her.

It turned out that Jean-Baptiste might be a world-class surgeon but, contrary to newspaper talk he wasn't a particularly nice man when he chose. Briefly, she imagined telling the world what the man behind the mask was really like. But no one would ever believe her. Jean-Baptiste was an institution. If she dared to openly criticise him they'd be more likely to turn on *her*.

It was a cruel twist that now, before she'd even had time to lick her wounds, Louis Delaroche—the one man now left who had it in his power to help her, but who never would—should have taken it on himself to deal with her. Crueller still that she couldn't silence the little voice inside her that kept reminding her of that glimpse of a caring, driven Louis to which she'd so recently been privy.

But surely it was a false hope to think she could turn to Louis? Just because she'd recently seen just how deeply he cared for his patients didn't mean he would care about Rainbow House. Or that he would care about anything the Delaroche Foundation did. At the end of the day, he was still a playboy.

Work hard, play harder, that was Louis's motto. His were never mere parties but Saturnalias; he never merely drank, he caroused.

Why, face to face with him now, did it seem so difficult to remember that side of his character?

Even now, as she tilted her head to take him in, his famously solid figure now framed by the light spilling onto the balcony from the French doors behind him, she wasn't sure what to make of him.

Louis was the man who the media simply revelled in loathing. Not least because his weekly exploits—both sexual and otherwise—sold copies by their millions the world over. Since his mid-teens, Louis had been building a reputation for being larger than life with a penchant for the kind of wild parties the average person couldn't even imagine. The scandalous occasion he and his rich friends had stolen one of their parents' super-yachts for a raucous party, only to subsequently sink it, was probably one of the tamer of Louis's outings.

And he got away with it all because he was one of the most gifted young surgeons of his generation. Women wanted him and men wanted to be him. Was it any wonder his ego was as gargantuan as the rather crudely reputed size of a rather specific part of his anatomy?

Well, she wasn't going to be yet another addition to the lusting harem that had trailed around after him all evening. Neither did she have the energy for an unwanted fight with another Delaroche male this evening.

Shock still resonated through her, but something else followed it. Something stronger. An inner core strength that had got her through losing her mother and her brother. Had got her through a lifetime of disappointing her father since birth. Got her to med school, to pass top of her year, and to the placements she'd wanted most.

She would *not* cry in front of Louis. She'd already been the object of one unwarranted Delaroche temper this evening, and she'd be damned if she'd let another Delaroche take his pound of flesh, too. Steeling herself, she raised her chin to look up into the dark shadow of a face she didn't need to see to have imprinted in her mind.

'Thank you for rescuing me from the humiliation of being thrown out in front of the press waiting outside, but you have…people to get back to.

And if you don't mind, I'll find a back way out of here and get safely home before your father realises I didn't get *made an example of.*'

'I don't think so.' His voice was lethally quiet. 'You still haven't told me why you were discussing Rainbow House.'

Frustration lent her courage and she let out a humourless laugh.

'The fact that you don't even know says it all.'

He took a sudden step towards her and made a sound somewhere between a growl and…*something*, his lips curving upwards into a shape so razor sharp it could hardly be called a smile.

Awareness shot through her, her heart thundering almost painfully in her chest. Her senses all immediately went on high alert, the stunning crispness of the cool night fading into nothing compared to the man in front of her. A reminder of why Louis was one of the world's most powerful eligible bachelors.

She gripped the rough stone surface of the ornate balcony tighter and it was all she could do not to back away further. To hold her ground rather than tumble over the edge. He was too distracting. A six-foot-three package of corded muscles, so lean and powerful and strong, its beauty was almost too much. No amount of scandalous headlines or scurrilous articles could have prepared her for the effect of being this close to Louis in person. And alone with him.

Not even the proximity the previous week when her mentor had granted her coveted entry into one of Louis's surgeries.

The moment when she'd seen Louis's incredible surgical skill for herself. The moment she'd seen a different side to the heinous media image when he'd shown such care and kindness to his patient and their family. And evidently the moment she'd begun to lose her grip on reality, for pity's sake.

Some small sense of self-preservation pounded inside her and she let out a disdainful, if somewhat nervous huff.

'Remind me, what *is* the collective noun for a group of immaculately coiffured, designer-ballgown-dressed, primly preening women who spend all evening zealously clamouring around a less-than-selfless playboy?'

'I believe they're called high-society contacts.' He flashed a wolfish smile that was more bared teeth and another shard of awareness sliced straight through her. Mercifully, Louis appeared oblivious. 'This is a charity ball, after all. I'm sure even you must understand that the aim is to raise as much money as possible.'

'I hardly think it's the charities they're here for,' Alex scoffed, recalling the covetous expressions on a sea of female faces when Louis had abandoned them in the ballroom in favour of her.

Only *he* could have made several hundred women look on with more envy than interest as he'd snatched her from his father's security detail, only to frogmarch her away, back through the vast estate house and finally here outside in the relative privacy of one of the many ornate stone balconies.

No doubt he thought she should be grateful to him for that much, Alex grumbled to herself as she rubbed her elbow and told herself that it was only tingly from the pain of Louis's grip. Certainly not the thrill of his touch.

That would be lunacy.

'I don't care who or what brought them here.' Louis shrugged. 'As long as they support the Delaroche Foundation. The sooner they part with their surplus money, the sooner I can say I've done my filial duty and get out of here. Which brings me right back to why you were discussing Rainbow House with my father.'

He advanced on her again, her feeling of suffocation nothing to do with the lacy choker at her throat. Because even without the name or the heritage there would never have been any denying Louis Delaroche. He carried himself in the kind of autocratic and exacting way that many men tried to emulate but few could ever master. For Louis, it seemed effortless, an intrinsic part of who he was. He only had to murmur 'Jump' and those around him would frantically turn themselves inside out to become metaphorical pole-vaulters.

Alex sniffed indelicately. Well, his ubiquitous charm wasn't going to work on her. She was determined about *that.* How ironic it would be if, after a life of trying to do the right thing, striving to be somebody worthy of living in this world, someone who could maybe one day make a difference, she should be toppled by something as prosaic as falling for the proverbial *bad boy.*

Even now Alex could imagine the sadness on her father's face. The knowledge that he'd been right about her all along. That she was worthless. That it was laughable she should have gone into medicine, a profession in which she was supposed to *save* lives when she only ever destroyed lives. *Their lives.* Her mother's and her brother's.

Mum and Jack. Or *them,* as she'd come to think of them. Grief slid over her, as a familiar as a set of scrubs yet in many ways equally as impersonal.

Not that her father ever blamed her aloud. Never made such an accusation. Never once even breathed it. Rather, it was the fact that he'd always been careful *never*, ever to mention it—never, ever mention *them*—that screamed louder than anything he could have said.

He was always so careful, her father, to keep subject matter defined. Work was fine, personal life was a no-go. Rainbow House was the only thing the two of them shared that had any connection to Mum and Jack at all.

And so her father must feel it, deep down. That kernel of loathing that she felt for herself. Rainbow House was the one good thing they shared. She *had* to save it. Whatever the cost.

That last thought helped her to steel her spine again. Lifting her head, she met Louis's stare head on, refusing to be distracted, however tempting the packaging had turned out to be.

'Rainbow House is a place for children with life-changing illnesses and their parents,' she informed him. 'A place that helps as many children as possible to find a cure, and offers respite for those who can't get the solution they need, whether it's a transplant or an operation. It sends families on that one precious memory-making holiday together, and helps fulfil as many bucket-list wishes as possible. Just the kind of place the Delaroche Foundation is famous for supporting.'

'I know what it is,' Louis remarked wryly, but the edge to his voice cautioned her.

Was she missing something? What?

'I asked why you were discussing it with Jean… my father,' he interrupted her musing, his voice sharp.

'I'd have thought you should be one of the first people to know what was going on at Rainbow House,' she snapped. 'But since you don't, here it is. Your precious Delaroche Foundation is trying to shut it down.'

'It is not my precious foundation. And even if it was, Rainbow House is part of the Lefebvre Group.'

'Which was bequeathed to you,' she announced triumphantly, ignoring the part where he'd known about the group. She wasn't sure what to make of it. Louis was hardly renowned for being interested in anything other than surgeries and sex.

Although, for all his vices, he kept his great obsessions clear and distinct from one another.

She had to give him that much.

'It was bequeathed to me as a kid. But the group has been doing a fine job of governing itself without me stepping in and wasting my time. I operate, or I party. I don't have time for charity as well.'

She couldn't fathom the expression that pulled tight across his face. As though his words didn't match his feelings on the matter. All of a sudden she remembered the Louis she'd seen in the operating room barely a month earlier.

She'd heard the stories about Louis's skill as a surgeon ever since she'd been a medical student. Only a couple of years older than her, he was already years ahead of his peers, apparently having observed his father's surgeries ever since he'd been old enough to stand on a box long enough in the OR. It was said that schoolboy Louis had been able to answer questions even second-year house officers had struggled with.

But last week had been the first—the only—time she had actually witnessed Louis in action for herself. It had been an incredible experience.

Louis didn't simply measure up to the stories,

he surpassed them. A surgeon of such skill and focus that he eclipsed any other surgeon she'd seen. And when she'd mentioned it to her mentor—the anaesthetist who must have promised Louis the earth in order to get him to allow her in to observe in one of Louis's infamously closed-door surgeries—Gordon had merely rewarded her with one of his conspicuously rare smiles.

She'd finally seen what Gordon had known for years, that Louis was a pretty unique surgeon. The more she'd run back over the surgery all week, the more she'd realised that it hadn't been luck that the entire procedure had gone so smoothly, so without complication. Louis had made so many tiny, almost imperceptible adjustments so instinctively throughout the operation that he'd headed off any little bumps before they'd even had a chance to develop.

Some surgeons reacted well to incidents in the OR, others were a couple of moves ahead. Louis, though she hadn't realised it immediately, was akin to a chess grandmaster who could foresee multiple patterns ahead and then made the best single move, even if it wasn't the most obvious one.

She might even go so far as to say Louis was

gifted. And after years of feeling proud—perhaps maybe even a little superior—that she was immune to some of the best-looking but arrogant doctors she'd worked with throughout her career, it was galling to realise that, of all people, playboy Louis Delaroche should be the man to breach her defences.

Not that she was about to let him know it. She rolled her eyes at him and pressed on.

'You're wrong. The board isn't doing a *fine* job at all. As I understand it, the Lefebvre Group is now almost wholly comprised of the Delaroche Foundation, ever since the death of the old chairman a few months ago. Your father's foundation has been voting to transfer various assets from the Lefebvre Group to the Delaroche Foundation, at very advantageous prices.'

'They can't do that.'

'Tell that to the board,' she spat back. 'Some of these assets they intend to keep and some they want to shut down or sell off. Rainbow House is located in the centre of town, it's prime real estate. Shut it down and any developer would pay millions for the site.'

'No.' Louis folded his arms over his body, the move only highlighting the powerful muscles there. 'That won't be why he wants to shut Rainbow House down.'

'You're telling me he has no choice?' She dragged her gaze back to his shadowed face. 'Because I can't believe that.'

'I didn't say that he didn't have a choice. I said he isn't driven by the money.'

Disappointment bubbled up inside her. She couldn't explain why she'd imagined she'd sensed a possible ally in Louis, but watching it slip from her grasp was almost like watching her own father slip away from her. They amounted to the same thing.

'Seriously? You, of all people, are now claiming he's philanthropic after all?'

'I'm not claiming anything. I'm simply telling you that selling the site for millions won't be the reason he's closing it down.'

'It's a much-needed centre. It benefits hundreds and hundreds of children and their families. We work hard to raise our own funds and we don't ask much more of the Delaroche Foundation than lending their name to it.'

In that instant it was as though everything around them had frozen, leaving only the two of them locked together in some kind of void.

'You work there?'

'Yes.'

'Why?' The question came out of nowhere. Not a challenge but a soft demand. Unexpectedly astute. Unavoidable. As though he knew she had to have a personal connection.

She couldn't explain it, she only knew—somehow—that it wouldn't pay to lie to him.

'I volunteer there,' Alex began hesitantly. 'With my father. My brother was… Years ago…we used Rainbow House.'

'Your brother?' Louis demanded sharply.

She flicked out a tongue over her lips, managing a stiff nod of confirmation.

'Yes. Jack.'

'And now?' His voice softened a fraction, he sounded almost empathetic. A flashback to the Louis who only usually emerged for his patients.

If anything, that just made it harder for her to keep her emotions in check. Alex fought to keep her voice even, the air winding its way around her.

'He died. Twenty-one years ago. He was eleven. I was eight.'

'I'm sorry.'

Simple. Sincere. And all the more touching for it.

'Thank you.'

Instantly the air finished winding its way around her and instead began slowly constricting her. Like a python immobilising its prey. And she felt she was sinking into the depths of those rich-coloured eyes.

She fought to control her heart as it hammered so loudly within her ribcage that he must surely be able to hear it. And then abruptly, rather than suffocating her, the silence seemed to cloak them, drawing them a little closer together and almost suggesting an intimacy that hadn't been there before. She realised she was holding her breath, not wanting to break the spell.

Funny, because she was usually so quick to move conversations on from talking about her brother.

'So that's why Rainbow House means so much to you.'

'Right,' she agreed, shutting off the little voice that urged her to tell him about her father.

Where did that come from? That was no one else's business but her and her father's. Certainly not Louis's. She lifted her head, determined to throw it back onto him.

'I suppose that's why I don't understand why

Rainbow House doesn't mean as much to you. Given what it meant to your mother.'

The icy change was instantaneous. She might as well have struck him physically. He reacted as though she had. Reeling backwards before he could stop himself, even as he recovered his composure.

'I don't know what that means. So when is this closure supposed to be taking place?'

It all happened so fast that anyone else might have missed it. They probably would have. But she wasn't anyone. It was her skill for observing the little things, picking up on the faintest of shifts, whether in patient symptoms, monitor readings or merely attitude, which made her particularly good at her job. A skill in which she had always taken such pride.

Right now, it was an unexpected glimpse of the less-than-perfect image of Louis that he carefully hid from eager media eyes. She couldn't help pressing him.

'It means I know your mother was Celine Lefebvre, and I know it was your maternal family who founded Rainbow House over fifty years ago when your aunt, your mother's younger sister, was diagnosed with childhood leukaemia.'

'How quaint that you know a little of my family history.'

His voice was as fascinating yet deadly as the ninja stars that her brother had always dreamed of one day being able to master. A dangerous cocktail of sadness, frustration and desperate hope flooded through her.

'I also know that your mother fought hard to keep Rainbow House open over twenty-five years ago when original Lefebvre Group members who had been appointed were running it into the ground. That was around the time she convinced your father to set up the Delaroche Foundation and oversee the group until you were of an age to take control. I'm guessing that she expected to train you to run it but…she never got the opportunity.'

'Which means it's nothing to do with me now.'

She wished more than anything she could decipher that expression behind his concrete-coloured eyes. But the longer she stared into them, the more unreachable he seemed to be. Her voice rose in desperation.

'She left control of Lefebvre Group to you. You could stop the foundation from doing this. Surely, for the sake of her memory, it shouldn't be so far beneath your concern?'

'Careful.'

It was one word of caution and it shouldn't have sounded so menacing. So full of control. But it had, and Alex shivered, feeling the sharp edges of the stonework cutting into her fingers.

'Rainbow House meant everything to your mother. The stories people have about her are limitless. She's a legend with everyone I know there.'

He turned his face a fraction, inadvertently allowing the light from inside to illuminate him. But she wasn't prepared for the expression of pain that pulled his features tight. It sliced at something raw deep inside her, something that she'd spent decades trying to bury. She slammed it away before it could get to her.

'I have no intention of getting involved,' Louis bit out.

'Is that why you rescued me from your father, then?'

She could hear the quiver in her challenge, knew Louis could hear it, too. Still, she refused to back down.

'I didn't want to see you humiliated in front of the press. It wouldn't have made the Delaroche

Foundation look good, especially on such an important gala night.'

'Rubbish.'

She had no idea where her courage was suddenly stemming from, but she wasn't about to question it.

'You wanted to know why we were talking about Rainbow House. You can tell me you don't want to get involved all you like, but clearly you do want to. Clearly a part of you *needs* to.'

'How interesting that you appear to know me so well.' He flashed his teeth at her in another intimidating non-smile. 'Let me guess, you know that Jean-Baptiste and I don't get on so you think I'd be prepared to go up against him with the board because of some sentimentality over a place my mother once patronised.'

'It's more than that, and you know it.'

She valiantly ignored the way her heart somersaulted within her chest. The way his mannerisms spoke to something undefinable within her. A blasé attitude that masked a vulnerability he didn't want anyone to see.

No doubt anyone else would have believed him. He sold smouldering disinterest all too well and even she herself couldn't help but be drawn in.

Louis was stunning, and edgy, and utterly mesmerising. But she was sure she could see past the front. That particular emotional Achilles' heel was something she recognised only too easily.

'It's true that vastly exaggerated stories concerning some feud between Jean-Baptiste and me—his prodigal son—have been gleefully published by the press for almost a decade—'

'You mean two brilliant surgeons, bonded by blood, united by mutual contempt?' Alex cut across him. 'Yes, I might have heard something about that. It's a media favourite.'

'Indeed. But that doesn't mean I care enough to take on Rainbow House merely to thwart him. It would cut into my playboy lifestyle too much—surely you've read about that, too?'

'I think it's an act,' she heard herself state boldly. 'I think you and your father have been in competition for as long as you can remember. He's one of the most image-conscious men I've seen, and I think your infamous playboy routine was your way of sullying the Delaroche name.'

'Nice theory. And if it was true, I'd say it's a resounding success, wouldn't you?' He quirked an eyebrow as though she amused him.

But Alex wasn't finished yet.

'Ah, but it hasn't worked as well as you'd hoped, has it? Because as much as the media love to hate you, they also hate to love you. If they ever realised quite how much you care for your patients, I think they'd be having bank holidays in your honour. No wonder you keep such a close-knit team around you—can't have people realising you're actually a good guy underneath that bad-boy exterior.'

Something skittered over Louis's face.

'And that fantastical notion is what you're basing your hopes on? You're relying on some non-existent version of me to save Rainbow House?'

'Why not?' She shot him an over-bright smile. If he was her last chance then she might as well go down fighting. 'Besides, it's not such a fantastical notion if I'm not the only one who thinks you could save the place.'

She had him. She could see it. And it gave her a thrill to realise she had hooked him so easily. But reeling him in, that was going to be the impossible part.

'Go on then,' he conceded, and she had to give him credit for not trying to disguise his intrigue.

'Half of your board.'

'Allow me to let you onto a little secret. Even if I wanted to save the place, I couldn't.'

'You could. All you have to do is take over control from the Delaroche Foundation, the way your mother always intended you to do.'

'Are you always this argumentative?' His lips twitched and Alex wrinkled her nose.

'I'm not arguing, I'm only pointing out—'

'So it's just me, then? I suppose I should take it as a compliment that I get under your skin.'

'You do *not* get under my skin,' Alex huffed, before realising that her fists were clenched into balls, hidden as they were by Louis's jacket. 'Well, if you do then it's only because I find it frustrating that you could help us—that you spend your professional life saving people, even if your personal life is in the gutter—and yet you stand on the sidelines and refuse to get involved.'

'You've got it all wrong,' Louis bit out. 'You're looking at me like some kind of white knight, but there's a reason Jean-Baptiste has that reputation and I don't. Besides, as I was saying before, I couldn't help you even if I wanted to. My mother might have left control of Rainbow House—or, more to the point, the Lefebvre Group—to me in her will, but not before my father had her insert a clause making one further stipulation.'

'Stipulation?'

'I have to be married.'

'Married? You?'

He simply shrugged. 'Quite. So you see there's no point looking to me to rescue you. Unless you care to marry me then I'm the last person who can help you.'

CHAPTER TWO

'YOU MUST BE DRUNK.' The disdainful wrinkle of her nose cut him far more than it should. 'As usual.'

'Most probably,' he lied smoothly, knowing he couldn't blame her low opinion of him entirely on the media.

But the truth was that he hadn't had a drink in months, maybe even the best part of a year. And even then it had been a rare brandy with a close friend. Ironic how easily water could be mistaken for vodka, if that was what aligned better with people's assumptions.

Strange thing was that he hadn't missed the alcohol or the wild parties. The latter had never made him feel any less alone, whilst the former had never even made a dent in the block of ice that had encased his heart for as long as he could remember. Or at least ever since his mother's… *death*. But, then, he'd never wanted it to.

Until recently.

If he'd been able to foresee how his first few dates with the it-girls of the moment would have resulted in a sex story that would define his playboy reputation for the next decade and a half, he might have thought twice about something that had been meant to be *harmless, private fun.*

Now it proved impossible to change. People didn't want to see him grow up.

Worse, he couldn't be bothered to prove it to them.

'Nonetheless, a marriage clause remains,' he proclaimed. 'And clearly I don't intend to satisfy that particular parameter.'

'Oh, but that's ridiculous!' the woman exclaimed, *sotto voce*, wrenching him mercifully back from the precipice of memory. 'I know the Delaroche family can trace its ancestry back to thirteenth-century aristocracy, with a palace for a family home, but this is the twenty-first century. Why would they have put such a clause in?'

'Perhaps for the very reason of thwarting you now.' Louis grinned, enjoying the way she flailed her arms around in frustration.

'Very amusing.' She glowered at him.

'Thank you.' He tried for modesty, but not very hard. 'And it's twelfth century.'

'Pardon?'

'Twelfth-century aristocracy, not thirteenth. And it isn't a palace but a chateau which, quite frankly, is mostly cold and draughty despite the modern improvements. We do, however, have a moat and a drawbridge.'

'As so many of us do.' She affected a deep sigh but her eyes twinkled and sparkled, and made him feel so much more *alive* than he had felt in…a long time.

He shifted to the side slightly to allow the light from inside to fall on her face. Pretty, wholesome, yet with a mouth that he wondered if she realised was as sinful as it was. He watched in absorbed fascination as emotions danced across her features like any one of the ballets he'd accompanied his mother to on the promise of an afternoon of ice cream and activity of his choice. But it had never been a chore, for either of them.

She'd been fun like that, his mother. And they'd been close. Or at least he thought they had been. He still found it hard to accept that she'd taken her own life. Had chosen to leave him. Even now, when he thought back over his life, those first seven years with her were still in vibrant Technicolor. He could even still hear her laughter, so unrestrained, so frequent. And then she'd…gone, and everything since had just been different hues of black and grey. Only his surgeries gave him that same feeling of invincibility.

And now this woman, whose name he didn't even know, had streaked into his life with a burst of colour and he couldn't explain it.

'You know, you could get married if you wanted to,' she said, a note of desperation in her tone.

'I beg your pardon?'

'Don't look at me like I'm mad.' She scrunched up her face. 'But you could. Any one of those women down there would leap at the chance to marry you.'

'Are you suggesting I get married just to inherit control of a place I don't even care about?'

'You do care,' she pointed out. 'You wouldn't have rescued me from your father or indeed still be here, talking to me about it, if a part of you didn't care.'

'You're mistaken.' Louis frowned. 'And as for the idea of marriage, you really think it would be morally just to inflict *playboy me* on any woman?'

She actually snorted at him. No one had ever done that in his life. She was either very brave or very foolish.

He found he was intrigued to discover which it was.

'If you put the idea out there, I can see a whole host of volunteers ready to play the part just to be married to Louis Delaroche.'

'Is that so?'

'That's so.' She nodded firmly and he tried not to let his eyes slide to the way it made her breasts jiggle in that sexy sheath of a dress.

Man, what was wrong with him? *Jiggle?* Really?

'It's honestly that simple,' she insisted, dragging him back to the present. 'You get married and the Lefebvre Group passes to you.'

'I'm sorry,' he couldn't help but tease her, 'you're putting *marriage* and *me* into the same sentence and you're calling it simple?'

She wrinkled her nose again and the guileless, girlish mannerism shot straight to his sex. So different from the manipulative females he'd been dating for too long. Who he was better off dating, because they were as jaded as he was.

Alex wasn't jaded.

Alex was vibrant, and direct, and he felt as though she was breathing new life into him.

He should leave now. Before he sucked all the life *out* of her.

'And how about you?' He dropped his voice to a whiskey-gruff tone.

Unable to quash the urge to seduce her.

It worked, as he'd known it would. If she glowed any brighter, one of the helicopters bringing guests in to the ball might have mistaken her for a helipad beacon.

'Sorry?'

'How about you? Would you be prepared to play the part, just for me to save Rainbow House?'

He told himself he'd meant it as a joke, to see how far he could push her. He suspected that wasn't the real reason.

'Not if you were the last hope for mankind.'

She tipped her chin up with defiance, meeting his gaze as though she was completely immune to the obvious attraction that sparked and cracked between them. But he knew how to read people, how to read women, and the staining on her cheeks revealed that she wasn't as unaffected as she pretended to be.

'It seems you have me at a disadvantage.' He held his hands palms up in placation. 'Since you know who I am, while, regrettably, I don't know who you are, shall we start over, this time with introductions?'

She narrowed her eyes, apparently searching for a catch. Her breath was still coming out a little raggedly. He took care not to focus on it. Or the way her pulse flickered at the base of her throat in a way that seemed to scrape inside him.

'Alexandra Vardy,' she acknowledged at length, although her tone was clearly still defensive. 'Alex.'

'Alex, then,' he replied. Then frowned. 'Alex Vardy? I know that name.'

She appeared pleasantly surprised despite herself, even if she subsequently shook her head, as though it didn't make any difference.

'I was in your surgery last week.'

'I don't think so,' he challenged her. 'My surgeries are strictly closed-door procedures. I attract too much press interest. The last thing my patients need are journalists sneaking in because they can watch one of my surgeries without being challenged.'

'The cervical cerclage on the woman with the twenty-week-old foetus,' Alex answered softly.

He raised his eyebrows, scrutinising the woman again.

'Indeed. Well, since you were in my surgery, for the record, her name was Gigi Reed. And she'd already named her unborn baby Ruby, just in case.'

'You remember their names?'

'It was a difficult case.'

'Not for you.' She eyed him anew. As though reassessing him.

Louis gave himself a metaphorical kick. He shouldn't have let her know he knew his patients' names. Gifted but arrogant, that was his reputation and he was fine with that. He didn't need anyone outside his trusted team to realise that he could probably name every patient he'd ever operated on, as well as linking them to their procedure.

What was it about this woman that fired him up the way she did?

People mattered to him. His patients mattered. They always had.

'The additional complications in this case and the fact that the woman turned out to be such a high-profile businessman's daughter have made it a high-interest story.' He went for one of his famous shrugs. 'Hard to forget her name.'

'Except that Ruby's name has never been mentioned.'

She didn't let up, this woman. He shouldn't find her tenacity so appealing.

'Fine, you've got me. I remember my patients' names. They matter to me. Their procedures matter to me. And Gigi's was a good operation. She'd suffered three miscarriages in the past, probably what had weakened her cervix. Stitching it closed might help prevent premature labour.'

He didn't add that the procedure carried significant risks, or that every minute, hour, day was crucial. He didn't need to. Alex clearly understood that or she wouldn't have been in his OR. The question was, who had let her in, and did some heads need to roll?

'It's a hail-Mary procedure that very few surgeons could have even attempted. Fewer still could have actually pulled it off.'

She bit her tongue before she could add whatever else it was she had been about to say. He found himself strangely curious. About what this woman…what Alex thought of him? He eyed her thoughtfully. Finally breaking free of her spell, falling back on what he knew best.

He advanced on her, watching with grim satisfaction as she braced herself, her eyes darkening with the mutual attraction she clearly didn't want to acknowledge.

'So you're Gordon's protégé.'

Another humble blush.

'I wouldn't put it quite that way.'

'I would.' His eyes never left her. He took another step towards her, watching her every reaction. 'He speaks exceptionally highly of you. He really fought your case for you to be in that surgery. I don't just let anyone in, you know.'

Was he still talking about his surgeries, he wondered, or had the conversation suddenly split off into a second, less overt direction? When had he let that happen? He deliberately advanced again.

'You should.' She almost covered the slight quake in her voice and he flashed another wolfish grin. 'You're an exceptional surgeon—any doctor would be inspired by watching you.'

The unexpected compliment caught him off guard. Why did it mean more when it came from this stranger's lips?

'Should I be offended that you sound so surprised?' he drawled in an effort to conceal his rare unsettled state. 'I understood my reputation as far as my career went was exemplary.'

The hollow, unimpressed laugh unbalanced him

even further and Louis didn't know what to think. He was always in control, always so assured that he found this current state of flux anathema.

'True, but with your hand-picked teams and closed surgeries, which most of us mere mortals have never actually witnessed in person, you'll forgive us for considering that your shining reputation could have been coloured by the simple fact that you're a Delaroche.'

'Is that so?'

'It is.' She affected a shrug. 'There's only one thing I don't understand.'

'Oh, and what's that?'

'The Delaroche Foundation has been given credit for the entire Gigi Reed procedure in the press. His name might not have been mentioned outright but the leaked article in the paper certainly made it appear that Jean-Baptiste was the surgeon, not you. Yet neither you nor any of your close-knit team has bothered to set the record straight.'

Why was it suddenly so hard to shrug it off as he would have had no trouble doing had anyone else been asking him?

'It's good for the Delaroche brand.'

The line his father had fed him since he'd performed his first exciting surgery. Jean-Baptiste's successes were his own. Louis's successes were those of the foundation.

And he didn't care. Because, really, what else could his father take from him that he hadn't already taken? Plus more accolades meant more expectation, which in turn meant more responsibility. And up until recently he'd been content with just his surgeries and his hedonistic lifestyle, as the media seemed so fond of calling it.

'I've heard you say that before.' She glanced at him astutely. 'To the press. How many times have you passed up taking credit for something that would have improved your godawful reputation with the media?'

'What if I don't want to improve my reputation? What if my playboy label gets me more… *benefits* than getting the credit for weird surgeries ever would? Besides, despite everything, I already have a good reputation with the media as a surgeon, so why worry about more?'

'Given how well documented your sexual exploits have been in the media over the past decade, it's a miracle you even know what day it is half of the time. Shame. I heard from Gordon that you were a decent enough lad in your late teens.

A bit arrogant, conceding that you were in med school while other kids your age were still doing their A Levels. Then suddenly you turned into the player of the century.'

He arched one eyebrow in quasi-amusement and watched her swallow once, twice. The sexual tension between them was unrelenting.

'And you wonder why my father reacted as he did. Are you always this combative?'

'I wasn't at all combative with your father,' Alex retorted hotly. 'I'm not a confrontational person.'

'I find that hard to believe.' Although, as it happened, he didn't find it hard to believe at all.

The mutual attraction was messing with his head almost as much.

He folded his arms across his chest, as if entertained. A move that he knew from experience only enhanced the strong muscles in his chest, his biceps, even his forearms. Muscles he had acquired through serious hours pounding the streets or in his home gym in a futile effort to exhaust himself into sleep pretty much whenever he had time on his hands and no stupid party to distract his racing thoughts.

Despite her obvious inner fight, Louis watched

as Alex tracked his every movement with her eyes, lingering longer than he knew she wanted to.

'So you're Apple Pie Alex.'

'I've never liked that nickname,' she bit out.

He ignored her, knowing his amusement only riled her up even more and wondering why he felt so compelled to keep pushing her as he was.

'Why do you suppose your colleagues call you that? Because you're wholesome and sweet, or because you're boring?'

For some reason, it cut right through her even though she tried not to let him see it. Instead, she rolled her eyes with a hefty dose of melodrama to distract him.

'Because apparently I'm comforting. Just like my grandmother's recipe for apple pie, which I foolishly brought in one day.'

'Comforting?' His chuckle rumbled out of nowhere. When was the last time he'd wanted to tease in this way? 'What? In the same way that a tankful of piranhas is comforting?'

'I'm very even tempered,' she snapped.

'I can see that. And for your next trick…?'

It was intended as a gentle ribbing, but by the expression on Alex's face she was genuinely struggling with her supposedly out-of-character attitude. He felt chastened, and yet he got a thrill out of this verbal sparring with her.

'I was polite and respectful with your father,' Alex said firmly.

'So, like I pointed out earlier, it's just me.'

'Yes.' She nodded, making him grin again, much to her chagrin. 'No. Oh, you're impossible. I just meant that I'm more on edge now, after… your father.'

'You're even cuter when your temper flares.'

'And you're condescending.'

'So I've been told,' he replied, unfazed. 'Many, many times before.'

'We're just going around in circles here, aren't we?' she said through gritted teeth. Then abruptly pushed off the balcony and sashayed past him, apparently tired of the conversation.

He wasn't sure that anyone had ever tired of a conversation with him before. Certainly they'd never walked away from him. He felt something like admiration surge inside him. As well as something more recognisable. Like lust.

'Come, now,' he admonished. 'You can't really be leaving. You haven't even heard how I plan to help.'

She didn't even turn around, merely slowed her

walk and cast her head over one delectably bare shoulder.

'So you finally *do* plan to help? That's a start, I suppose. All you need now is to return to your harem and decide which one of them you'd prefer to join you in no doubt unholy matrimony.'

'Oh, I've already decided that.'

'Really?' She spun around in surprise. 'You really are going to do this, then?'

It was just that Alex was a challenge, Louis told himself. And normally he would relish the challenge. All too often he would have beautiful women falling over each other to throw themselves at him. He wasn't proud of the fact that he indulged, frequently and indiscriminately, but it had suited his bad-boy reputation and he'd often told himself that he was just a red-blooded male like any other. But sometimes a challenge was fun. Especially if it came in the kind of package standing in front of him and pretending she wasn't fighting the chemistry sizzling between them.

But right now wasn't normal.

It all came back to the name he hadn't heard in years. Decades even.

Rainbow House.

He'd thought about it more tonight than he

had in all the last years combined, banishing it from his head to the pitch-black depths of nothing, with all the other painful memories of the happy life before his mother had gone from it. But what had pretending it didn't exist accomplished? His mother was still gone and Rainbow House had been one of her legacies. Even decades on it shouldn't amaze him that his old man was still trying to erase every last one of them.

For the first time Louis had a compulsion to stop him. To save at least one good thing his mother had achieved. He told himself it had nothing to do with the captivating woman currently gliding away from him. He couldn't explain why Alex talking about the place should reinvigorate it with such colour, such life. He only knew he wasn't ready to relinquish it—relinquish *her*—just yet.

'I've made my choice, but I might need your help,' he announced gravely, watching her take a single step back to him almost against her will.

'My help?'

'Sure.' He strode towards her, supressing a grin at the way she flicked a tongue out so deliciously over her lips. 'You don't think it's going to be easy for me to get any potential father-in-law to agree to giving me their daughter's hand in marriage?'

The closer he got, the more she leaned the top half of her body away from him. But her feet remained planted in place, almost as if her head was telling her to back away but her body was telling her something quite different.

He knew the feeling.

'Oh, come on.' She gave a bark of laughter. 'You can't really expect me to believe you'd do something so chivalrous?'

'Why not?'

'Because…well, because…you're you.'

'Nice that you noticed.' He really shouldn't be enjoying himself this much. 'But as it happens, I do like the odd tradition now and then. My family is, as you say, traceable back to the twelfth century.'

'You don't say?' She widened her eyes in mock surprise. 'Then surely any potential father-in-law would be falling over themselves to literally throw their daughters into your arms. Particularly the classy women you date.'

'I'm shocked that you would cast such aspersions, Dr Vardy. Nonetheless, I have the distinct suspicion that it was matter of charming half of their daughters into bed out of wedlock that must have turned them against me in the first instance.'

'Only half?' she quipped tartly. Too tartly.

'No, well, one can't be too greedy.' He shrugged dismissively, neatly changing the subject. 'Of course, you appreciate that the more you lean back from me the more you angle your hips towards me? One might even say *invitingly.*'

Her eyes widened, her scowl deepening, and she faltered backwards just as he'd known she would, giving him the perfect opportunity to reach forward and halt her fall, hauling her body closer to his as he did so.

'You did that deliberately,' she said irritably, though he noticed that for all her objection she remained in the light circle of his arm, though she could have pushed him away if she'd really wanted to.

It only served to fuel Louis's desire. He could tell himself that this was all part of his plan and that he was still in control, but he knew that somewhere along the line, that had ceased to be entirely true. He could no more explain this attraction as he could fight it. He'd been attracted to women—plenty of women, though nowhere near in the disgusting numbers that the papers so deliriously hypothesised—but never like this. Never on a level that he knew wasn't merely about the physical.

'I can't seem to help myself,' he drawled, his tone intended to conceal just how unexpectedly close to the truth that statement was.

Even now, as his eyes took in the rapid pulse at her neck, the stain of lust spreading over her skin, the sudden huskiness in her voice, doing something as simple as drawing a breath suddenly became an arduous hindrance.

He leaned forward and she stepped back. Right up against the stone balustrade, allowing him to place an arm on each side and effectively cage her.

'What are you doing?' she whispered. Hardly a protestation of his position. Still, he needed to be sure.

'Making sure you don't run away.'

'I'm not running away.' He recognised that hoarse desire in her voice. He'd heard it plenty of times before. But never with anyone who made him as hard as she did.

Like he was some hormone-charged teenager.

'You know my reputation,' he ground out. 'You should be running.'

'I know your reputation,' she concurred. 'But right now I don't know anyone else who can help me stop your father.'

It was hardly the rebuttal he realised a part of

him had been hoping for. As if he hoped she might see past the bad-boy exterior to the honourable man he knew had probably died a long time ago.

Pathetic really.

Louis had never wanted, never sought anyone else's approval. He would leave that to his father. Though how he was the only person to see through his old man's veneer to see that he'd only set up the Delaroche Foundation as a way to earn himself a knighthood, he would never understand. Let Jean-Baptiste revel in his unearned glories as much as the vainglorious old man wanted.

His mother would surely laugh out loud to know that Rainbow House was still a thorn in her husband's side. Even now.

It was only when he caught Alex watching him curiously, his arms still trapping her in place, that he remembered himself, and banished the unwelcome thoughts from his head.

He pushed backwards, releasing her with a theatrical flourish, exultant when she didn't go anywhere.

'So, Dr Alexandra Vardy, how about it?' He flashed her a wolfish smile, playing the habitually drunk playboy role for all he was worth. After all, why else would a bad boy like him make such a ridiculous suggestion? 'Want to marry me and stop my father from committing any more of his dastardly deeds?'

CHAPTER THREE

'SOMEONE PAGED ME?' Louis burst through the doors of the pre-op room, taking in the unfolding events in one careful sweep.

'I did. I suspect an anaphylactic reaction in your patient,' Alex answered quickly but calmly, her attention going straight back to the patient in front of her even as she addressed the anaesthetic technician. 'Freddie, let's set up an IV. Start with eight milligrams of dexamethasone and point one milligrams of adrenalin.'

'What happened?' Louis stepped over quickly without, she just had time to notice, getting in the way of her staff.

Surprisingly he didn't wade in, but waited silently for her to finish issuing her brief, perfunctory instructions to her team.

It could be no coincidence that she had suddenly been assigned as part of Louis's on-call team tonight. She'd been avoiding him for two days since she'd walked—though she still had no idea how her legs had kept her upright after his audacious marriage suggestion—away from away him.

Clearly, this was his way of flexing his authoritative muscle. An irrefutable demonstration of the power he wielded in this hospital. She'd spent the last few hours enacting scenarios in her head in which she had confronted him about it. But right now it definitely wasn't the time.

'The patient was clearly hypovolaemic when she was brought in,' Alex informed him. 'She was clammy in appearance and tachycardic.'

'She presented in the emergency department a couple of hours ago following a salpingo-oophorectomy three days ago,' confirmed Louis. 'All signs led the resus team to suspect intra-abdominal bleeding, which was when they referred her to us.'

Cool, professional, approachable. No hint that he even remembered what had happened between them on that balcony. How she had been within a hair's breadth of kissing him, of letting him kiss her. If he'd pushed it that tiny bit further, she knew she would have.

Every spare moment since, she'd wondered why he hadn't.

Was it insane that every time she'd thought of him, a gurgle of laughter had rumbled within her?

The thing about arrogant men was that they had altogether too high an opinion of themselves to be likeable.

Yet Louis was wholly unaffected by his stark male beauty, and he didn't take himself too seriously. He made her laugh.

It didn't fit.

Still, she couldn't afford to dwell on it. Forget her illicit fantasies about him, he was standing right in front of her, right now, and he was all professional. The way she always prided herself on being.

She pulled her head back in the game, relieved to realise that she hadn't missed a beat.

'Yes, I completed the handover twenty minutes ago. She appeared calm despite the circumstances. Blood pressure was one-twenty over seventy and heart rate was eighty-four beats per minute. Intravenous access was difficult, probably as a result of the hypovolaemia and the suspected internal bleeding, but she did have a cannula in situ, which we used.'

'You used it for general anaesthetic induction?'

'Right, then we intubated.' Alex nodded. 'There was an initial delay of results for the carbon dioxide output but the tubes were in correctly, there was misting and the chest was rising symmetrically. I began manual ventilation, which I thought felt restricted, and when I listened to her chest I heard wheezing. I had already started to suspect anaesthesia-related anaphylaxis, which was when I told them to alert you to the situation.'

There had been no need for Louis to come in. As the anaesthetist, this was within her remit rather than his, but she could understand why he wanted to see for himself. In many respects she was still an unknown quantity to his team. Typically Louis.

'You're using her foot—?'

'To gain additional venous access? Yes,' Alex cut in, straightening up with a satisfied nod and taking the bag of colloid fluid from her team. 'Good. Right, let's start infusing and get her blood pressure back up and her cardiovascular volume. Freddie, start drawing up another point one milligrams of adrenalin.'

But before she could get much further the patient went into cardiac arrest.

'I'll start compressions.' Louis moved instinctively to the table, allowing her to continue administering the adrenalin.

They both knew that while in ordinary circumstances the surgical procedure would be called to a halt, due to the acute nature of the internal bleeding, it wasn't an option in this situation. She had no choice but to get it under control.

Good thing she'd never been one to crumble under pressure.

Still, it was a relief when Louis confirmed cardiac output had been regained and Alex was able to insert both a central and femoral line, even as she issued further instructions to her team to treat the anaphylaxis before continuing their pre-op procedures.

'You're re-administering anaesthesia?' He frowned, still watching her closely.

Her pride kicked in. She couldn't help it.

'I thought I might.' The tongue-in-cheek tone was clear but now the patient was stable, and after the tension the team had been under a little dark humour always worked to buoy morale. It was just the way hospitals seemed to work, in her opinion.

It wouldn't make the team work any better to keep stress levels high. Still, she kept her eyes on the monitoring equipment as she spoke.

'If it's internal bleeding then I can't imagine you could afford to postpone the operation, and with all the excitement the last thing the patient needs is to come out of the anaesthetic in mid-operation, wouldn't you agree?'

'Never preferable,' he agreed, as she concluded her tasks and gave him a slight nod. 'We're ready?'

'Ready,' she confirmed, knowing that, even if the surgery was carried out quickly and without incident, the post-operative management was going to be crucial.

It was going to be a long night. And yet, when the patient came out of it treated and cared for, it made it feel like the best job in the world.

If only she didn't have Louis to deal with at the end of it.

'Good call on the anaphylaxis case.'

Alex visibly stiffened as he called to her from across the atrium. It was a deliberate ploy on his part so she couldn't continue to duck out, having pretended not to see him, as she had been doing for the last nine hours.

And the atrium was the perfect trap. During the day it was a bustling hub of staff, visitors and mobile patients. Right now, it was relatively deserted, save for the trio around Alex's small table. It was one of the reasons he'd chosen this moment to corner her, when the fewest people were gawking. But she didn't need to know that.

Let her think he hadn't considered her at all.

He couldn't disappoint that way.

He sipped his coffee and sauntered deliberately over to where they sat, pulling out a chair and sliding down easily into it. Alex barely glanced up as the over-eager pair began falling over each other to introduce themselves to him, and he politely acknowledged them then affected insouciance, all the while taking in every possible detail.

By the expressions and body language of the group he'd lay a bet that the two women had barely socialised with Alex before yesterday's papers had come out, and more specifically the grainy, pixelated image of him escorting her out of the kitchen entrance of the gala event the other night—clearly taken by one of the kitchen staff on their mobile phone, he was already dealing with them—and suddenly Alex had become everyone's new best friend.

Another thing he was guilty of.

Louis managed to smooth out the grim expression before it could settle on his lips. He refused to apologise or feel remorse. It had been him or being publicly ejected through the main doors by the security team. Though she'd probably have been the first woman to choose the security team after his outlandish proposal to her.

There was no reason for him to still be grinning about it.

'Ladies, it's a pleasure to meet you but I wonder if Alex and I could have moment?'

She sucked in her breath audibly and he knew what was coming the moment the women left the room. Sure enough, as soon as the doors slammed Alex practically exploded.

'Oh, why don't you just drive a tanker of fuel into the damned fire?' she seethed. 'They'll be gossiping all over the hospital as we speak.'

'Isn't that the idea?' He grinned. 'Generate publicity and all that.'

Her eyes narrowed.

'The papers are already speculating, thanks to that photo,' she hissed. 'Grubby little rumours about how I'm the latest notch on your bedpost.'

'Ah, well, the quicker you agree to marry me, the less *grubby* they can make it. The story will go international and you'll be the woman who tamed me.'

'No woman will ever tame you,' she snorted. From anyone else he would have taken it to be a compliment, but for some reason her contempt needled at him.

He pointedly ramped up his grin.

'Of course not. But the story is bigger if they think you have. And the more publicity the more chance we can help Rainbow House before my father gets his way.'

She frowned.

'I thought that if you got married, you got control of the Lefebvre Group and then Rainbow House and others like it would be safe anyway.'

'You might think that,' he agreed, carefully concealing his amusement that she'd just revealed she had actually been considering it, despite her rather vocal rejection of the idea last night. 'But I've been looking into the specific clauses ever since the gala. It seems that unless we get married before the official vote on any transfers then any such decisions will still carry through.'

'For pity's sake.' A torn expression contorted her face.

So this was what it felt like to be such a heel, putting more pressure on her than she already had. But, then, she was the one asking for *his* help. She just needed to set her prejudice against him aside for long enough to agree this was the only way given the short timeframe she'd given him.

Not that he really blamed her for her vacillation. He'd hardly set himself up to be keen to help.

The sound of her fingers drumming on the plastic table echoed in the vaulted space.

'Why?' she demanded abruptly.

'Why what?' It was a feeble attempt to stall but her question had caught him off guard.

'Why do you want to help Rainbow House at all?' She eyed him shrewdly. 'You didn't when I first asked you. And then said you did but really it was all a joke to you. Yet suddenly you're getting me onto your surgical team and trying to collar me in public places. So, what's going on?'

Louis arched one brow.

'You know what they say. It's a surgeon's prerogative to change his mind.'

'No one says that, Louis.'

'I do.'

'Yeah, well, as far as I'm concerned, you don't count.'

He feigned a hurt expression.

'You cut me to the quick.'

'I highly doubt it. But if I did, I suspect that with the number of women literally falling over themselves to bag you, I'm sure you'll get over it remarkably quickly.' She crossed her arms over her chest and he resisted the impulse to tell her that the action only thrust those pert breasts of hers to the fore.

He could save winding her up with that one for another day. Right now he was enjoying the show too much. Namely the *Feisty Alex* routine; so far removed from the wholesome *Apple Pie Alex* but which, now he'd done a little digging, he'd discovered was a closely guarded fact amongst a select handful of her closest friends, Gordon being one of them.

What did it say about him that he actually *wished* to be part of Alex's select circle?

'So, should I take that as your answer then?'

He snapped back to the present.

'Say again?'

'I asked why you really wanted to help me suddenly. You chose to deflect in your usual manner.'

'You don't pull any punches, do you?' His grin widened.

'With you? No. I don't think I can afford to.'

'I like that,' he mused, taking another long swig of his coffee. She might want something from him but she wasn't about to pander to him. He was all too accustomed to people pandering to his wishes. Not least in the bedroom. 'That why I think you'd be the perfect marriage choice.'

'I'm flattered,' she drawled. 'So why not tell me why you're so fixated on your marriage idea all of a sudden.'

'It wasn't my plan,' he reminded her smoothly. 'It was *your* plan. You're the one who asked me to help. And you're the one who suggested I get married simply to satisfy the clause in my mother's will.'

'Well...yes,' Alex faltered. 'But...but not to *me*.'

'You really want me to inflict this charade on some other woman?'

Why was he enjoying this quite so much?

'I doubt they'd feel remotely *inflicted on*,' she sniffed. 'While for my part, my picture is in the paper as your latest lover. One of hundreds if the papers are to be believed. My reputation is, for want of a better word, tarnished.'

'All the more reason for you to agree to marry me.' He shrugged.

'I don't know.' She toyed with the paper cup, long fingers playing with the corner of card, unpeeling it carefully, meticulously. 'You're right, I wanted your help but I was desperate. I suppose a part of me never thought you'd agree to it. And now you have… I can't help but wonder why.'

'Does it matter?' he wondered aloud.

'Yes. Are you motivated by getting one up on your father in this ridiculous game the two of you seem to be permanently playing?'

'Does *that* matter?'

'Yes, Louis, it does. Because you're infamous for being a loose cannon and if I have any hope of controlling you then I need to know what sets you off.'

'Now I can definitely tell you *that,*' he countered suggestively.

'Louis…' Alex sighed, a soft sound as though he actually *exasperated* her.

And suddenly he didn't want to play the charade with her any longer. He was exhausted with playing up to perceptions of how he should be. All he wanted to do was kick back and let the mask slip.

'Louis,' she bit out abruptly. 'Is this about getting your own back on your father?'

He should lie. Come up with another typical quip. Instead, he heard himself respond.

'Maybe. A little. You know, before last night I hadn't thought about Rainbow House in years. Did you know I usually travelled with her? Backwards and forwards between Chateau Rochepont and the UK? Did you also know that Rainbow House is where my mother died?'

Died; suicide. Pot-ay-to; pot-ah-to.

He tried to stuff back the pain he'd thought long since buried. Play it down as he had in the past. But, for once, it didn't seem to fit back in its dark, wretched cage. Instead, he plastered a smile on his mouth and pretended he didn't hear the way Alex had sucked in a breath and shot him a look of pure horror.

'I didn't know that.' Somehow that made him feel better. 'Is that why you haven't taken on her legacy all these years?'

'Partly.'

He hadn't been able to bear it. Taking on the legacy of a woman who could have achieved so much more. Who had chosen to take her own life when she could have followed her passion for the Lefebvre Trust; who had chosen to leave her desperate, seven-year-old son behind.

His only consolation was the fact that only he and his father, and whoever had discovered her that day, knew the truth. It wasn't in anyone's best interests to disclose such facts. The last thing Rainbow House would have wanted was negative media attention. Covering up his mother's suicide had been the one decent thing his father had ever done. And even that hadn't been for altruistic purposes.

'Her name was Celine, but you already know that.' He had no idea why he was still speaking. Why he was telling her things he'd never uttered to another soul. But it was like a faulty tap and now he'd opened the faucet he couldn't shut it off again.

'She didn't have the greatest life. She was pretty but rather naïve when she met Jean-Baptiste. By the time she found herself pregnant with me, she was nineteen. My grandfather on my father's side was only too keen to unite two aristocratic families while my grandfather on my mother's side believed that Jean-Baptiste was doing the honourable thing in marrying Celine.'

'And that was a bad thing?' Alex was cautious.

'With hindsight my mother was too young, too innocent to handle a man like my father. She would have been better off without him, but an unmarried pregnant woman was still a scandalous thing, especially in this area, back then. My grandfather just wanted to be sure that Celine and her son and rightful heir to the Delaroche estate—me—would be acknowledged.'

'Were you close?'

'Very.' And suddenly he was fighting off a slew of unwelcome emotions. It was enough to evoke so many memories, but he would *not* remember her soft voice, her contagious laugh or the fresh scent of her hair when she'd hugged him. He would not remember how they'd spent every single day together, out on walks along the section of Canal du Midi where the chateau was, or collecting pine cones in the surrounding woods. And he would not remember how she'd taught him about the birds and their songs, only for *him* to have to teach *her* all over again when he was six and had discovered she'd got it all wrong.

He *could* not remember it. He'd long since found that detonating those flashbacks in the deepest, darkest caverns of his soul had been the most effective way to eradicate them.

'Jean-Baptiste was as vile a husband as he was a father.' Louis flipped the subject quickly. 'What you saw that night is only a glimpse of it. He's a bully and a coercer. Gradually, systematically, he beat my mother down until she felt she was worthless.'

'She couldn't leave him?'

'We talked about it. We agreed how different life would be without Jean-Baptiste's money or connections, and we concluded how much easier it would be to breathe without his restrictions. That last trip to Rainbow House was to be her final one. When she flew back we were going to leave. Then she…died.'

He understood why she'd had to be free of his father, but he could never forgive her for choosing such a way out. For not simply packing a bag for them both and fleeing in the dead of night. For leaving him behind.

'I'm sorry for your loss, Louis.'

Her words wrenched him out of whatever black pit he'd been sliding into. He fell silent, old grief washing over him. And then, for the first time, a hint of something resembling a soothing calm.

He stared at Alex.

Was that because of her? He couldn't be sure.

She was watching him warily. Opening her mouth, then hesitating and closing it again.

'What is it, Alex?'

She bit her lip.

'For what it's worth, your father isn't as loved by

the Delaroche board as you, or the media, seem to think.'

He didn't know what flooded through him then. 'What do you mean?'

'It means there are some members of the Delaroche board who would like nothing more than to see your father ousted.'

'That's absurd.'

She shook her head.

'No, it isn't. I told you, I've been working at Rainbow House for over a decade. People talk. People talk to me. There are quite a few people who had seen that other side of your father, the one the press seem oblivious to. I hadn't believed it until I saw for myself the other night. But if you came back, Louis…if you took control of the Lefebvre Group, I think there may be quite a few members who would support your nomination within the Delaroche board as well.'

'But you don't know for sure.'

Why did he even care? He had his surgeries, and when he wasn't at the hospital he had his hedonistic lifestyle. He didn't want anything to do with either the Lefebvre Group or the Delaroche Foundation. He didn't belong in that world. He should stick to what he did best.

Except something niggled at him.

He thrust it away.

Alex had asked for his assistance and, though he couldn't explain why, he wanted to help her. Wanted to make sure she and her father kept the fragile connection between them, the link to her brother. The kind he had never had with his own father, and had lost with the death of Celine.

'If you want to save Rainbow House then you're still going to have to marry me.'

'There has to be another way. Your position in full control of the group can't really be wholly dependent on whether you're married or not.'

'Only it is. And, yes, I could probably fight the clause if I wanted to. Get a top legal team and find some way around it, but it would take time. And I don't think Rainbow House has that time. Not if the vote to transfer is imminent.'

'Which means you have to get married imminently,' she said.

'Right. So, Alexandra Vardy, how much does Rainbow House really mean to you?'

It was a bit of a loaded question, he recognised that as soon as he asked it. But rather than another of her wisecracks, she shot him a sideways look.

'It means more than I could tell you. I just don't know if we can pull this off.'

'You doubt me?'

She heaved a deep sigh.

'No, as it happens. I've seen how driven and focussed you can be. What you can achieve when you want to. I just don't know if you want Rainbow House enough.'

'Well, you're going to have to make a decision.' He felt unbalanced. Intoxicated. Her decision had been like an intimate caress to the hardest part of his masculinity. Nothing like the fawning, gushing compliments that so often peppered his day yet meant absolutely nothing to him.

'You can trust me and maybe we can save Rainbow House, or you can fail to trust me and we save nothing.'

The last thing he expected was her sudden wry grin.

'Hobson's choice, then.'

Whether she'd intended it or not, it had the effect of chasing away the uncharacteristic melancholy that had threatened to sweep through him. He suspected she understood that, which was why she'd chosen to back away.

It should bother him more that she'd been able

to read him so easily when he prided himself on the fact that no one else ever could.

'It is. Although regrettably I don't have an extensive stable of horses.'

She laughed, and the sound cascaded through him like a pleasant waterfall.

'You can't really expect me to believe that. Only the other night you told me that your family home is a castle. You truly don't have huge stables?'

'The stables are long gone. Or at least the horses are gone and the stables have seen better days. They're not really a priority for my father. Does that count?'

'And what about the media? Do you think you'll need to get them onside?'

'Possibly. Which I think is where you would come in. I think you'd be the perfect person to charm them.'

'Wow, thanks, I'll look forward to it.' She pulled a face. 'So you think they'll believe you're no longer the fickle, play-hard womaniser Louis who has never dated a woman longer than about a week in his life, just by taking a girlfriend…sorry, I mean a fiancée?'

'Why not?' he murmured. 'Eligible playboy

bachelor tamed by sweet girl next door, it's an age-old story and people love it.'

It should be a cliché. But if it was then he was staring right at half of it.

'I'm not the girl next door,' she snapped, before softening her words with a smile. But it was more brittle than those that had gone before. And the sudden change snagged his attention.

He wanted to know more about Alex, and she'd just given him the ideal opening.

As though sensing a chink in her armour, Louis suddenly leaned closer and abruptly the huge, vaulted space felt as claustrophobic as a three-by-three tent. The seductive Louis was back, edging closer, and even sitting down his body was definitely one built for sin. Heat swept through her afresh but she ordered herself not to be such a fool, not to fall for it. It was simply an act he knew how to play to perfection.

'Then who are you, Alexandra?'

The too-sharp edge to his gaze unnerved her, the attraction still zipping between them. Inconvenient and undeniable. One misstep and she got the impression he could convince her to lay her soul bare. She wanted to get back to the banter they'd had before but she had to tread carefully.

'So, Louis…' She forced a smile, buying herself a little more time. 'If I did agree to marry you, how do I know you'll honour your promise to me about Rainbow House?'

'You have my word.' He shrugged, making her splutter. Her eyebrows shot up to her hair.

'That's it? The word of a renowned playboy.'

'I might have a reputation as a playboy, but shouldn't that make me honest rather than a liar? I never promise women something I can't give them.'

'Is there anything you can't give women?' she said, regretting it the moment it came out of her mouth. It would only inflate his already giant ego.

'I appreciate the vote of confidence.' His crooked smile *did* things to her. 'And you're right. There's only one thing.'

'And what's that.'

'Marriage,' he deadpanned. 'Commitment.'

'Idiot.' She actually swatted him. She waited for him to react but he just ramped up the killer grin.

'I deliver in all other areas.'

'So I've heard. You have quite the reputation for delivering.'

'Indeed I do. Care to put it to the test?'

Her whole body reacted, thrumming at the soft teasing of his tone. Grey eyes pierced into her like the short, sharp scratch of a needle into a vein. The air between them appeared to crackle. His eyes locked onto hers and she couldn't make herself break contact.

'I'm harder to dislike than you thought, aren't I?' he teased.

'You keep telling yourself that,' she bit back, but it lacked any edge.

And here they were, full circle. He *was* harder to dislike than she'd believed from his media reputation, she'd been learning that over the last few days. In fact, the more time she spent in his company, the harder it was to see the two sides of him as the same man. She sniffed delicately.

'So if we want to get married then first we have to get the media invested in your apparent redemption.'

If Louis flinched at the term, he recovered quickly.

'That's the plan,' he agreed. 'Although, full disclosure, there's nothing remotely redeemable about him left any more. Too many years of playing the wild, arrogant playboy have meant my soul has long since been sold.'

For a moment she wondered if he truly believed that. There was such an odd tilt to his expression. And then it was gone.

Still, she felt compelled to answer.

'If Jean-Baptiste can convince the press and public alike that he's some kind of benevolent force, then I'm sure you, too, can learn to play the part.'

'Don't tell me that was a compliment.'

Before she realised it, he leaned forward, his fingers sweeping over her forearm. The fleeting contact was electrifying.

'Take it,' she suggested, wishing her voice didn't sound quite so husky. 'It's the best you're getting.'

'Oh, no, trust me. You'll be doing way better than that before the ink is dry on this so-called marriage. Many of them comparing me to a deity, just as you're reaching orgasm.'

Why was it that every time she thought she'd struck a nerve with Louis, he came back more scurrilous than ever? Was it his way of concealing some vulnerability, or was she just imagining something that wasn't there?

Either way, she had to stop reacting to him, stop taking the bait.

'I haven't even agreed to it yet.'

'But you want to.' Hard, male triumph. 'Finally we're getting there. Tell me, what exactly do you have to lose?'

She stared at him for a moment, wishing she could read his thoughts and then wondering why she cared so much.

It didn't make sense.

'My soul, perhaps?' she offered.

And maybe something else she didn't care to admit.

He laughed, and then suddenly he leaned in. And she found herself wondering what she would do if he closed the gap and kissed her. He was so close, so big, so… *Louis.* Even his teasing had made her body hum with desire.

If he kissed her then she had a feeling she would kiss him back.

And then she would hate herself for it.

For that reason alone, she pulled away and forced herself to stand up.

'You will come to me, Alex,' he murmured, so quietly that at first she wasn't sure if it was just the thoughts in her head, taunting her. Knowing what she was trying to tell her body it didn't want.

'I won't.'

'Oh, you will. And when you do, you'll come willingly. Eagerly. And I'll be waiting.'

'This has to be a business arrangement, Louis. Not for pleasure. We have to set out the ground rules now.'

'Why not for both?' he asked, low and sensual. 'We'll discuss it tonight. Over dinner. Where the press can see us and we can start the clock ticking. The car will collect you at eight. Be ready, Alex. Don't keep me waiting.'

CHAPTER FOUR

THE NIGHT WAS not going as planned.

True, the press were outside, tipped off by an *anonymous source,* as arranged. And he had pre-ordered the soufflé to suggest that he had given this date care and forethought. But the so-called date itself hadn't gone as intended.

He was too distracted, too fascinated by the woman who was sitting opposite him.

He should have spent the last hour discussing with her the next steps in their plan. Instead, he'd spent it watching her, studying her, trying to learn about her. She was a breed apart from any other women he'd previously…entertained. Not just because she was a doctor, and the kind of skilled anaesthetist he should have known Gordon would want to mentor, but because of *her.* Because there was something about the woman that he found utterly compelling.

She was driven and she was focussed, both qualities he'd never looked for in a lover before.

Qualities, if he was honest, that he'd gone out of his way to avoid. Sex was simple, but cerebral attraction was a complication he could do without. And there was no doubt he found Alex Vardy utterly desirable; physically and otherwise.

As if sensing his scrutiny, she lifted her eyes, a scowl knitting her forehead. When she pursed her mouth he was helpless from imagining dragging his thumb over that plump lower lip, dipping his head to taste the sweet heat of her mouth, pulling her body close against his. It was nonsensical. And pathetic. And it made him feel like the kind of hormone-ravaged teenager lusting over the hottest girl in school he'd never been.

Yet here he was. Imagining.

'Do you have to look at me in quite that way?' she grumbled suddenly.

'Sorry?' He flashed her the slow, easy smile that women never failed to respond to.

Alex, however, appeared less than impressed.

'*That* way.' She waved her hand abstractedly in the air towards him. 'As though I'm some kind of puzzle box and you're trying to work me out.'

Another little nugget of information about her that he found himself seizing upon.

'You enjoy puzzle boxes?' He swirled the wine

around his glass. Experience told him the act in itself was enough to convince the casual observer he was drinking it.

'As it happens, yes,' she fired back. 'Though I've no doubt they would be considered too geeky for someone who prefers the kind of X-rated pursuits that you do.'

'I wouldn't write me off so quickly. You clearly have no idea how attractive geeky can be.'

'Right.' Had she really rolled her eyes at him? 'Because you're well known for your attraction to geeky women.'

The laugh rumbled low in his stomach. He loved these flashes of her feistier side, made him hungry to learn more. And that fact alone should bother him more than it did.

'I think the fact that you like puzzle boxes makes you all the more—what shall we say?—*interesting.*' His scrutiny deepened. 'Do you have a collection or something?'

She smoothed out the frown before it could crease her face, careful to keep her tone level.

'By the way, are you actually planning on drinking any wine? Or do you think by swirling it around the glass every now and then that I'm going to believe I'm not drinking alone?'

The corners of his mouth twitched involuntarily.

'I'm impressed. Most people wouldn't have noticed that fact.'

'I'm not most people.'

'No. You aren't.' He dipped his head to the side, relishing the stain that spread across her cheeks.

'Is that supposed to be a compliment?'

She was going for nonchalance but was clearly unpractised. Without her scrappy side, her innocence was even more endearing. Louis grinned.

'You know it is.'

A silence descended over their table and, while he was content just to watch her and assess, after a few moments Alex shifted awkwardly, glancing around the room. All about them couples were talking in low voices, laughing together, even cuddling in their booth-style seats. If the whole idea was that the press saw them together and began to wonder, surely the only question on their lips would be if they were even there together in the first instance?

'Shouldn't we be…doing something? Generating interest?'

Another wicked grin cracked his face. Why was it that she was so deliciously easy to bait?

'Nice to see you're suddenly so keen. What do

you suggest, then? Rampant sex underneath the table? The tabloids would go frantic for the chance to squeal to the world that I indulge my insatiable sexual needs in restaurants the length and breadth of the country.'

She pulled a face.

'Just the country? Surely you're ambitious enough to take on the world?'

Was it perverse that he got such a kick out of the fact she never seemed to let him get away with a thing? He dropped his voice to something approaching intimate, and leaned forward across the table to take her hand.

'Right, now, who says I'm not just interested in you?'

Far from delighting her, it earned him a withering glare from his companion.

'I bet you say that to all the girls.'

'True.' The accusation scratched its way under his skin despite his attempt to let it roll off him. Usually, it was a line delivered with considerably more aplomb. A truth in the face of irrefutable physical evidence.

'I also know that as much as you're pretending to want to pull your hand away, the flare in your eyes and the way your breath has quickened tell me that what bothers you most isn't that you don't want me touching you, but that a part of you is enjoying it far more than you think you should.'

Alex really defined the idea that beauty was more than just skin deep. He admired her passion. He admired her drive. He admired the lift of her head as she met his gaze proudly, the cool smile on her lips enough to fool the casual observer.

'You're mistaken, but then with an ego as big as yours that shouldn't surprise me. But I'm not pulling away because I know that if we go ahead with this charade then I can't afford to look like I'm not interested in you.'

'You keep telling yourself that. We can both feel the attraction here.'

His smile sharpened, tugging low in his stomach like a primal challenge.

'You're a pitiable Lothario.'

'I freely confess to the latter; however, I'm fairly sure no one's called me pitiable before.' He chuckled. 'At least, not to my face.'

'I'm equally sure you haven't been called plenty of things to your face,' Alex bantered quickly, 'but that doesn't mean you haven't been called them.'

Unperturbed, he lifted his wine glass to his lips

and prepared to take a sip, the hint of a smirk deliberately moulding his mouth.

'Oh, no doubt.'

There was no reason on earth for him to get such a kick out of bringing out a side of her that other people didn't seem to see.

'You really don't care at all, do you?'

There was also no reason for her disdain to needle him the way that it did. For him to go from amused to regretful. For it to suddenly be so hard for his practised smirk to stay in place.

Since he was seven years old he'd spent his life ensuring he *never* cared about what people thought. Because the only person whose opinion had ever mattered hadn't cared enough about him to stick around. People could say and think whatever they liked, it had never bothered him. If anything, it had been mildly entertaining.

There was no reason on earth why he should experience even a trickle of regret when he wondered how Alex might judge him.

'I didn't say that.'

'You didn't have to.' She was trying to sound scornful but it lacked the necessary bite. 'It's etched into every apathetic bone in your body.'

'I'm glad you've been paying so much attention.'

'You play up to those cameras, don't you? Give them the volatile Louis show they all love to see? Play the buffoon? And know you get away with it because half the female population seems to be in lust with you.'

It should antagonise him more. People simply didn't defy him. Instead, he found himself relishing her tenacity. Her refusal to be intimidated.

'You exaggerate your court-jester routine, your insouciance, and your sexual prowess.'

'Trust me, there's nothing remotely exaggerated about my sexual prowess.'

He savoured the way she flushed, the increased rise and fall of her chest, the darkening of her pupils, the faint flare of her nostrils. He told himself that he only cared because it would make it easier to deceive the paparazzi if there was at least a degree of genuine chemistry between the two of them.

He knew it was a lie.

'So,' she continued after a moment, 'this afternoon I told you why Rainbow House mattered to me when I told you about my brother Jack. Now you're going to tell me why Rainbow House is so important to you.'

It was his chance to redefine the parameters.

To remind her, and himself, that this was a business deal, nothing more; that she didn't have the right to demand anything of him. Louis opened his mouth to tell her, one of his well-honed put-downs ready on his lips.

His gaze swept over Alex's face. Sincere, open, ingenuous. Like no one he'd ever known before.

And for the second time in as many days he found himself opening up and letting the dark ghosts of his past emerge into the light for the very first time.

She hadn't expected him to answer. She'd thought he might brush it off, the way he always did when any of his work colleagues politely made personal enquiries. Or else make a scathing remark, as he did when the media prodded him considerably less politely.

Perhaps what startled her most was the way Louis shifted to face her square on in his seat, or maybe how he lowered his voice so that she had to edge in closer to hear, as though their conversation wasn't for the rest of the world to know. It might even have been the way he toyed with the pepper shaker in the middle of the table as though he was feeling suddenly, uncharacteristically, unsure of himself.

It was several long moments before she realised she'd stopped breathing.

'My mother didn't die in an accident at Rainbow House, the way everyone seems to think. She committed suicide.'

'That's ludicrous. My brother was in and out of the place around the time your mother died. He would have been around six, which means I was probably three. My father would have known.'

Her breath came out in a single whoosh. He ignored it, continuing with even less emotion than he had shown when choosing their expensive bottle of wine this evening.

'Have you ever thought about why, if she was such a hero in rescuing a place like Rainbow House from the brink, she isn't more celebrated by the centre? Why her connection to the charity has been all but erased? Why you only knew about her because your brother was a resident all those years ago, and because you still care enough to volunteer there now?'

'Well…yes. But…'

'No one talks about her. Certainly no one who

was around at the time. I'd lay a bet your father never mentions her.'

That was true. In fact, when she'd mentioned Celine and the Delaroche connection to her father, he'd ignored her. It was only when she'd mentioned her idea of attending the gala to speak to Jean-Baptiste that he'd snapped at her and told her not to be foolish. He, who wanted to save Rainbow House as much as she did.

'Nevertheless…'

'It happened, Alex.'

'How do you know?'

'My father told me at the time. Told me he'd managed to cover up the details surrounding her death and that as far as the press were concerned, there had been an accident.'

She heard the scornful snort; realised it was her.

'Your father?'

'I didn't want to believe it. I spent the best part of a decade telling myself it was a lie, and that one day I'd uncover the truth. I was seventeen by the time I was in a position to do that. I discovered that there had been no official police investigation, although an internal investigation had taken place with as few personnel as possible. A couple of them had since died, but no one left was talking. At least, they only confirmed the story that the press knew, none of which matched my father's all-too-vivid account.'

'Louis…' she began. She wanted to ask so many questions, wanted to comfort him. It was impossible to tell whether he would have accepted her sympathy or shut down again. She couldn't risk the latter. Gripping the table, she hardly even dared to blink.

'Most of the evidence had long since been destroyed. I barely managed to get hold of a few photos, which was all that remained. There was one of a ripped-up bedsheet, and my mother's favourite handbag, and the broken pearls from her necklace on the floor next to the beam they had cut to get her down. It all matched the story my father had told me. He hadn't been lying.'

'I can hardly believe it,' Alex offered tentatively. 'The woman I've always heard about from my father was so happy, so generous, so full of love.'

'She was. And, I suppose, for all his flaws I have to be grateful to my father for at least preserving her good reputation. Hushing up the details and ensuring the press reported nothing more than a tragic accident was the kindest thing he could ever have done for my mother.'

‘So…is that…’ She paused, thinking of all the best memories of her brother she’d clung to over the years. ‘Do you still remember the good times with her? How close you were?’

He shrugged and she couldn’t explain it, couldn’t justify it, but somehow she sensed that—far from the negligent attitude Louis had used to fool the press for so long—a maelstrom of feelings actually raged beneath the surface. Undetected by others, stuffed down by Louis.

‘I remember her leaving the chateau the previous night. She’d promised to take me with her because I loved the plane so much, but I was sick that day and she had to leave me behind. She told me she loved me, and that she would fly home as soon as she could. I waved to her out of the window as her car went down the drive. She even got out just before the moat and waved back. I never saw her again. Twenty-four hours later she’d taken her own life.’

‘Louis, I…’

Before she could finish, almost out of nowhere, the atmosphere changed and the razor-sharp, dominant veneer for which Louis was so famous slipped back into place.

'Ah, your chocolate soufflé. Savour it, I'm assured it's the best in Europe.'

The conversation was over and Louis was sampling his dessert and throwing compliments to the chef as if every mouthful wasn't sticking in his throat the way she knew it would have done for her.

But she wasn't fooled. He wasn't unmindful or unaffected. He simply didn't trust her. Alex wondered if he had ever trusted anyone.

How long had he isolated himself in this way?

As long as she had?

It shouldn't matter and it certainly shouldn't make a difference. But it did. She understood him better now, and what she'd learned had thrown her somewhat. He wasn't at all what she'd imagined, even with the twist of the surgeon she'd seen in action the previous month. Every time she saw him, spoke to him, it felt as though she was discovering a man no one else even knew existed. And even though she knew she should know better, she craved to learn more.

It was thrilling, and nerve-racking, and utterly bewildering. How was she supposed to react to everything he'd told her? She could barely even digest it all. She needed time, in particular to ensure that she wasn't at risk of losing all perspective and actually doing something as foolhardy and foolish as falling for the man.

But her biggest fear was that time wasn't a luxury she had right now.

The decadent dessert felt like wet concrete in his mouth. Worse, Alex was looking at him as though she could see straight through every bluff he cared to conjure. The way she had almost from that first encounter.

Still, he shouldn't have told her that. He shouldn't have told her any of it. If he could have shovelled back his words and rammed them all back inside then he would have.

Except that he wasn't sure that was even true.

No one had ever been able to read him the way she seemed to, a fact that ought to concern him far more than it did.

They finished their so-called date in strained silence. The only consolation was that, from all the covert glances and barely concealed smirks they were receiving, people were only too happy to draw their own, rather different conclusions.

For all her mental reservations about the two of them, Alex's body language right now betrayed the fact that on a purely physical level she was far less hesitant. Without the benefit of hearing their conversation, any casual observer would no doubt mistake her awkward fidgeting for eagerness to conclude the meal and get back to more private surroundings so they could continue the date on more intimate terms. Whether Alex liked it or not, she wasn't schooled enough in the art of seduction to mute the sexual attraction that crackled between them, blazing as brightly as a beacon warning of impending invasion.

The irony wasn't lost on Louis.

Neither was the fact that fooling the press into thinking they couldn't get enough of each other was only the first part of the plan. But the idea of *sex* and *Louis* was practically a given. What they really had to convince people of was that there was more to it than simply *sex*. They had to make the world believe the two of them shared a connection, an area of common ground. A foundation on which they were about to build a real relationship.

It should ring more alarm bells that he knew just how to snag Alex's focus.

'Did you enjoy your morning with our team? In the end?'

A man could quickly grow to love that wide, uninhibited smile. The one that told him she'd already forgotten herself. And their surroundings.

'I loved it,' she breathed. 'You get some incredible cases. Well, of course you do. But, I mean, you're one of most fascinating surgeons to observe. Your entire team is so well knit.'

'It's taken years to build the perfect unit, people with not only the skills I need but also the attitude I like. And the ability to leave all egos at the door.'

'Yes, I saw that.' Alex nodded, then blushed. 'Even you. I hadn't really expected that.'

'I'll take it as a compliment,' he commented wryly. 'I was impressed at just how easily you slotted into the team.'

'I did?' She looked inordinately pleased and something tugged inside him.

It felt good to compliment her. Especially as it was so well deserved.

'You were everything that Gordon said you were, and more.'

'I wondered if…?'

She leaned in eagerly, but whatever she was about to say died on her lips as several camera flashes went off.

Louis barely remembered standing up, much

less moving around the table. But one minute he was in his seat and the next he was pulling Alex to her feet, holding her close and ignoring the way she stiffened against him, while the staff ushered the photographers outside. It would only be later, on the drive home, that he would wonder at his instinctive reaction to protect her, shield her, when the entire point of the so-called date had been to flaunt their relationship to the world.

But for now, all that consumed him was the way Alex felt in his arms, her initial reticence already melting away as her body softened, curving into his, moulding herself to him. As if they had been designed to fit together.

'Let's go,' he muttered, waving the apologetic maître d' out of their way and tapping his watch and making a call to ensure his driver would be out front in a matter of minutes. Telling himself his body wasn't celebrating the way she pressed herself tightly against him.

'I can walk by myself,' she muttered, though she made no move to push away from him.

'But it would look better if you didn't want to,' countered Louis, refusing to acknowledge the voice suggesting he was motivated by more than just the way it looked to others. 'Better if you preferred to be in my arms.'

'But not like your typical Louis Delaroche date.' She shook her head, toying with the fabric of his shirt, as though she was willing her hands to brace against him and push him away.

'Isn't that the point? That you're meant to be unlike anyone I've been with before?'

'Still, like you said, I don't think wholesome, boring, grandmother's *Apple Pie Alex* is going to convince the press. Do you?' She barely gave him time to reply. 'If we want to convince people that you're a changed man, we need to give them a reason they'll believe. A spicy apple pie. The Apple Pie Martini.'

'Sorry, the what?'

But she didn't stop to answer.

Flattening her palms against his chest, Alex propelled herself back and pulled herself up to her full height, more like the confident, feisty woman he'd seen that first night. The smile she cast him shot straight through him and to his sex and then she spun around and glided out the doors and into a sea of camera flashes, appearing for all the world like she was born to a life in the spotlight. Part girl next door but part fierce Amazonian. It filled him with a sense of pride, of… almost *possessiveness.*

He couldn't explain it, all he did understand was that it meant the papers, once they found out who she really was, would be eating out of her hand in days. And that was before they saw the sheer drive and determination that governed her world.

How much more was there to Alexandra Vardy? What might he discover if he had the chance to peel back one skin after another? Why was he so damned intrigued by this one woman?

The questions jostled around his head with such eagerness that for a moment he almost forgot to follow her.

He, who never followed anyone.

Bursting through the doors, he covered the ground to her in a few long strides. Sliding his hand to the small of her back and guiding her the last feet to the kerb as their car headed towards them.

'Quite a show,' he murmured, leaning in to whisper in her ear, and exalting in the fact that only he could see her quickened, nervous breathing.

'I think it got the message across.'

'Perhaps. But a kiss would seal it.'

'I don't want to kiss you.'

'Liar,' he whispered, angling his head even closer to her ear so that her lips couldn't be seen by the cameras, but there was no mistaking the way her body trembled. It sent waves of desire through him. 'Love and lust are easily mistaken for each other. And there's no denying you and I have the latter. We both feel it.'

'I don't feel anything,' she refuted, but her voice lacked any conviction.

'Is that so?' he growled.

She was going to stall. Louis refused to give her the opportunity. He yanked her in, his mouth claiming hers and silencing any further objections.

Hot and glorious, and full of sinful promise. It wasn't like any other kiss he'd ever known. His mouth moved over hers, the whisper of her tongue against his fanning the flames that raged inside him. This was the kiss he'd been imagining all night.

Maybe even the kiss he'd been imagining his whole life.

As though she was the drink he'd never been able to find anywhere else, and the only one that could ever quench the thirst that had plagued him for what seemed like for ever. It wasn't just the way her tongue now scraped over his in sweet response. It wasn't just the way she tensed, relaxed, and then pressed against him, her breasts splayed against his body, generating a heat that burned right through clothing he desperately wished he could just rip off. It wasn't the way she tasted of need and longing and ultimately of promise.

It wasn't any of that. Yet it was all of it.

His head was spinning and, as hard as he tried, there was only one thought he could seem to hold onto.

He couldn't let her go. Not after this. He couldn't risk her backing away again. He liked this spiced version of Alex. Maybe a little bit too much.

When the car came, it was as much an interruption as a relief to break apart and bundle her inside.

The sudden silence was a jolt after the fracas out there.

'Where do you live?' Louis asked after a moment.

'Sorry?'

'What's your address?' He barely recognised the raw voice but it was hardly surprising when she was still trembling in his arms. And this time, he knew, it had nothing to do with the press.

'Why?'

'Because we're heading there now. You'll have half an hour, forty minutes at the most to pack everything you need and you'll move in with me.'

'I will not,' she squeaked.

He sighed. The sort of gently impatient sigh one might have bestowed on a small child who refused to hear what was being said to them. Alex would never know what it had cost him to rein himself in as he had.

She opened her mouth to speak but he cut in smoothly.

'You have no choice. Surely that's obvious to you?'

'Why should it be?' she challenged uncertainly.

'Because now the press have linked us, they're going to hound you until they get more. Camp out on your doorstep, harass your friends and relatives. You need to move somewhere it isn't as easy for them to gain access to you. Not only for your sake but also for the sake of your family.'

'I don't have a family.' The words were out before she could bite them back, as she clearly wished she could. She tried to pull out of his arms but he refused to let her. 'Just my father.'

'And your mother?'

She flinched, pressing her lips into a thin line, but at least she wasn't trying to pull away from him any longer. For the first time it occurred to Louis that he'd been so busy telling her things he'd never told anyone before that he hadn't thought to have her investigated as he usually would have. He vowed to remedy it as soon as he could.

'Either way, I'm sure you don't want him to see your every movement in the papers when they climb trees, or break into your back garden for the photos that capture a day in your life.'

He hated the way she recoiled from him.

'Oh, God, my father. He'll see photos of that kiss in the papers tomorrow.'

'And in the news tonight,' Louis pointed out gently.

She covered her face with her hands.

'It's what we wanted,' he reminded her. 'What we *needed* them to believe.'

It had just happened faster than he'd intended. And he couldn't pretend he'd been entirely in control. She had a way of making him act like a desperate kid. Either way, they'd set out their proverbial stall. Now they had to sell their wares, starting with ensuring she now moved in with him.

The car was pushing through the crowd and somehow he knew he needed to get her to agree now. Before the moment between them was broken.

'Put it this way, I have to go to France for a month or so. There are some cases that I've been waiting to complete out there. You'll be safer in my penthouse than on your own, but you won't have to worry about me seeing you with bed-hair.'

He took the snort to be a mirthless laugh. He didn't know why he was so suddenly desperate for her to agree. It wasn't just about making sure she was safe, he knew that. He suspected it was something far more primal. And that was dangerous.

'Alex?'

'Okay.' She dipped her head fractionally, clouds skittering across her eyes.

He could read the sense of foreboding that she desperately wanted to shake. Her feeling that she was somehow capitulating and that he had won. But it didn't feel like a win. He didn't know *what* this feeling was.

He only knew that the very ground was shifting precariously beneath his feet and it was all to do with this one woman.

Worse, Louis had no idea how to keep himself from plummeting into the void head first.

CHAPTER FIVE

'IT'S THE STUFF of spy movies, isn't it?' Alex was still struggling to regain her composure after the kiss as the plush lift whisked them silently from the underground garage to Louis's private penthouse.

'Sorry?'

She waved a negligent hand in the air, wondering if he could see the way it trembled, even now, at the memory of his mouth against hers.

'I mean, the exclusive key card to access the security pad just so you can enter in some private code. And that's before the lift had even closed its doors.'

Alex fought valiantly to appear light-hearted, but how could Louis fail to hear her heart drumming out its wild tattoo on her ribcage?

'That's what money buys,' he said with a shrug, that hint of darkness she was beginning to recognise meaning he'd have given it all up in a heartbeat just for one question to be answered. *Why his mother had chosen to do...what she had.*

It was a sense of helplessness that she understood only too well. It was getting easier and easier for her to read the man who had confounded the press for so many years. They had him pegged as this complex genius playboy.

They didn't understand him at all. And the two of them had a lot more in common than Louis realised.

She wasn't sure whether she'd realised it on the drive from the restaurant to her home, or from her home to here. But she'd realised it. She wasn't foolish enough to think that she'd worked out the entire puzzle box that was Louis Delaroche, but she'd at least figured out the first stage of him. He was as lost and hurt as she was, if for different reasons. And for each of them, that unbearable void couldn't be filled by another person and so they'd each been driven by their work.

That was why she felt such a connection with him. And in turn it explained why she'd acted so out of character outside the restaurant back there. Why she'd allowed herself to be kissed so thoroughly in front of a sea of flashing cameras. Why she'd come alive in his arms in a way she'd never before believed possible.

If only it was that simple.

If only she could pretend it really was just a mental connection rather than a physical one. How easy and convenient that would be. But there was more to it. It was less cerebral, more visceral. Louis fired up a need in her that she hadn't even known existed until he had come along. As if he had crept under her skin and infected her with some kind of thrilling fever.

And she liked it.

It didn't matter how many times she tried to tell herself that Louis had only kissed her to distract the press from her obvious gaucheness, she still craved more. Physically she felt drained and yet energised. She *ached* for him.

Lifting her fingers, Alex traced them lightly over her lips. She could still taste him on her mouth, feel his solid chest against her tender breasts, recall his strong hands tracing patterns up and down her spine.

In her whole life she'd always prided herself on her fight over flight attitude, but in this instance she knew if it hadn't been for Rainbow House she would have turned and run. She couldn't say how she knew it, but Louis Delaroche had the power to devastate her just as he'd devastated so many women before her. It turned out she wasn't as immune to that kind of man as she'd always assumed.

But, then, Louis wasn't *that kind* of anything. There were no others like him, he didn't so much break moulds as stick them on a mine and blow them to a grey mist.

So, here she was, in the lift to Louis's penthouse. And on top of all her roiling emotions it was difficult not to feel at least a little intimidated by Louis's obvious wealth and luxurious lifestyle. Especially when she thought of her own little flat and what he must have thought, pulling his flashy supercar into the communal car park packed with small older cars, scooters and a plethora of battered bicycles chained up together. A world away from the exclusive garage below, adorned with flashy cars recumbent in their generously proportioned, allocated parking spaces.

'Are you coming in?' The low voice broke through her reverie. 'Or do you intend to ride the lift all night?'

With a strangled sound Alex lurched forward, as if her legs didn't quite belong to her, and out of the lift to where Louis stood at the door to his penthouse. The edge in his voice accompanied by the hard, distant expression—as though he could read her thoughts on their kiss and scorned her for them—only made her fears swell.

And then she stepped past him into the room and everything rushed from her mind.

'That view is incredible,' she gasped.

One minute she was too close to Louis and the next she found herself across the room, palms flattened on a bank of glass looking out at the twinkling city as if she was somehow on top of the world. Or, at least, the closest she had ever come. The lights spread out for miles under a blanket of night and even some of the tallest buildings, which had always appeared enormous to her even from the fourth floor of the hospital, were now dwarfed by the breathtaking views from Louis's penthouse.

No wonder Louis walked, talked, acted as though the world was his for the taking. To him, it was.

'Is this how you seduce all your dates?' she asked, thinking that it really was a breath-taking view. 'All your *real* dates, that is?'

The pause stretched out for longer than was normal but when she turned, she wasn't prepared for the curve of his lips that developed into a full-blown smile of...*warmth?*

It blasted her, as though opening an incinerator door.

'I can't say any of my previous so-called dates have ever been interested in the view. Not the one out there, anyway.'

She shot him an exasperated look, and felt a little better.

If she had to work alongside Louis while such inappropriate longings poured through her then she needed to rediscover the light banter, the teasing back and forth they'd touched on earlier.

It was better than the alternative. Than the... kiss.

'Are you ever more impressed with anything other than your own brilliance?'

'Aren't you impressed by my...*brilliance*?' He quirked an eyebrow.

Something rolled and flipped low in her belly.

'I'm more astounded by your indefatigable arrogance.' She tried for loftiness but her own lips refused to do anything but curl upwards in amusement. His devilish grin of response wrecked her insides.

'Thank you.'

'It wasn't a compliment.'

'Oh, I would strongly disagree.' His rich, amused voice reverberated around her.

Abruptly, he moved to stand beside her, his head turned to the same view she saw, as if trying to see it through her eyes. She suspected he had long become immune to its beauty. She wasn't prepared for him to grow so quiet and serious.

'But, to answer your original question, lots of things impress me. Even astound me. Especially the strength of some people's human spirit inside and outside my OR. What you told me about your life back at the restaurant.'

His unexpected compliment made her yearn for more. Alex clenched her fists against the glass, silently cursing such weakness.

'There was nothing impressive or astounding about my life. People have it far worse.'

'And many don't. Either way, few of them use it to drive them on to becoming the star pupil of one of the most sought-after anaesthetists in the country, let alone the hospital.'

She could barely think straight, let alone talk.

'That was just work. And a bit of luck.'

'That was *you*,' he corrected softly. 'You asked

if anything impressed me and you're right that few things do. But I'm telling you that you're one of them.'

She hated herself for the way her heart suddenly soared. If she wasn't careful, the press and the Delaroche Foundation board weren't going to be the only fools to fall for this charade.

She really was like a breath of fresh air.

He'd spent the entire drive fighting the urge to kiss her over and over again. To taste that delicious mouth from every angle. It had been like some kind of torture being so close to her and not allowing himself to indulge. And as for that interminably long ride in the lift…she could never know how close he'd come to hitting the emergency stop.

Yet now here he was, standing side by side with her and staring at the view as though seeing it properly for the first time in a long time—perhaps the first time ever—because of Alex. Because she was so genuine.

None of the women he'd ever brought up here had cared about the view. They weren't the kind of women who would ever have been interested in such simple beauty. But Alex wasn't similar to those women. She wasn't swayed by the superficial, she cared about the things that mattered, about people who mattered. She made *him* start to care again. Not about his patients—that was a given—but about something other than medicine. About Rainbow House.

He'd never thought anyone could make him do that.

He'd been fighting an attraction to her ever since that first night on the balcony. Even now, he couldn't stop himself from thinking how Alex could make a room light up just by walking into it, just as his mother had once done. Alex could make *him* light up. And he didn't want her to stop.

The realisation slammed into him with such force he felt as though every last bit of air had been sucked from his body. As though his lungs were crumpling in his chest. He wanted Alex. Not just to finally wrest his inheritance back from the Delaroche Foundation, as had once been his mother's intent, and not just to save Rainbow House from his father.

He wanted Alex because she made him feel. Something. Anything.

Not for ever, of course, because that would be nonsensical. He didn't *do* long-term relationships. He never had.

But for as long as this charade lasted, he wanted it to be more than simply a charade. He wanted it to be more…*real.* He wanted her.

Worse than that. He wanted to *know* her.

'What is it?' Alex touched his arm and he realised she must have repeated the question at least once.

He shouldn't answer. He should shrug it off. He certainly shouldn't indulge this fantasy of his of getting to know her as if they were in the kind of real relationship he'd always studiously avoided in the past.

'What is it about the view that so enraptures you?'

'I don't know.' She frowned, taking a step away from him. 'What is it usually about such a magnificent sight?'

Defensive. Just the way he'd surmised.

'When I was a kid my mother used to say that views like these made her feel as though the world was spread at my feet for the taking. That, standing in front of it like this, she believed I could do anything.'

'You're a Delaroche, the world *is* yours for the taking,' Alex countered, but her words lacked any real heat.

'I couldn't control everything, though,' he said quietly. 'Any more than you could with your brother. Jack, did you call him?'

A momentary pang of guilt made its way through Louis as he watched her turn stiffly back to the window, her fingers braced against the glass as she stared out mutely.

'Do you volunteer at Rainbow House because you want to, or because you feel you somehow owe it to your father?'

'Because I want to, of course,' she snapped automatically.

He didn't bite, but neither was he about to let her off that easily.

'Is that really all there is to it?'

Her knuckles paled as she pressed her fingers down harder. As though some internal battle was going on in her head. Louis could imagine what it was only too easily.

'Perhaps a bit of both.' The admission came through gritted teeth.

'You feel responsible for your father's happiness? Responsible for Jack's death?'

'It's complicated.'

'It often is.' He couldn't explain why his heart twisted for her. 'But it doesn't always have to be.'

Her head was fixed away from him, her gaze trained on the vista below. But he would lay a bet she wasn't seeing any of it. Not a single building, or road, or tree. The haunted expression hovering over her beautiful profile betrayed her otherwise calm exterior.

'You don't understand.'

'So enlighten me.' He knew he was pushing. He couldn't seem to help himself. 'I can refute as many clichés as you can come up with, Alex.'

And then she smiled. A soft half-smile that looked more sad than anything else. But she turned her head and she finally looked at him.

'Jack was my older brother. He was diagnosed with diamond blackfan anaemia aged two. They tried other treatments that didn't work. I was conceived shortly afterwards in the hope that my stem cells would save him.'

'You were a saviour sibling,' Louis realised abruptly.

'Back before the time when embryos could be checked for compatibility. It was a leap of faith for my parents.'

'Alex, I had no idea.'

'It didn't pay off,' Alex continued, as though she hadn't heard him. 'Once I was born they carried out the tests and found I wasn't a match. Jack died seven years later.'

'I'm sorry,' he said simply.

The hush in the penthouse swirled softly around them.

'Your parents didn't try again?'

'My mother died when I was…a baby. They didn't get a chance.'

Her expression pulled tight and Louis couldn't shake the thought that he was missing something. Before he could say anything she was already speaking.

'I don't know what they would have done otherwise. Jack and my father had always been very close.'

He wanted to reach out and pull her into his arms. Comfort her. But he could read her well enough to know that she didn't want that. She might at least be looking at him, but her body was still steadfastly facing the world outside.

Strong. Resolute. Determined.

Apple Pie Alex indeed. Anyone who called her that didn't understand her at all. They completely missed that steel core that ran right through her from that blonde head to the soles of her feet.

The matching pair to the one which he'd always prided himself ran through him.

'So you volunteer at Rainbow House because your father does? Because you still feel responsible for not saving your brother?'

Quietness settled around them afresh before Alex finally answered.

'I suppose that's part of why I started. But I find it fulfilling.'

'And it's just you and your father?'

He wondered if her father had blamed her for not being able to save Jack. If the man had taken his grief out on his little daughter.

She narrowed her eyes at Louis. Too shrewd, he realised.

'Yes. It's just been the two of us ever since I was seven. And my childhood was fine, since I know that's what you're asking. My father loved me, in his own way, he supported me through university and with my career. We might not be as close as some families but he did lose his wife and son after all. It's hardly unusual that he might be a little closed off.'

'And you lost your mother and brother.'

He knew the words hit their mark. He could see her flinch. And he didn't know if he hated himself or her father more. Whether her old man had intended to hurt her not, he'd clearly withdrawn, taking demonstrative love with him.

She didn't need to say the words, he could read them all over her lovely face. Her father had fallen apart. Two people he'd loved most had gone. And instead of pouring that love into the one child he had left, he'd pulled away from her.

Her father might not have overtly said or done anything to hurt her, but clearly his absence of words had been almost as damaging. Certainly, Alex still felt she had something to prove to him. She was still the one fighting to keep their only area of communication alive. Fighting for Rainbow House.

At least he himself had experienced the unconditional love of his mother for the first seven years of his life. If Alex had lost her mother, and her father had known her brother's death had been inevitable once Alex wasn't a match, then had she ever experienced even that fraction of joy he'd had?

He doubted she'd thank him for pointing that out.

'Is that what got you started in medicine?'

'You mean, did the fact that I felt guilty about

not being able to save Jack drive me on to try to save as many other people as I could?'

'That isn't what I was asking, no.'

They both knew her reaction had revealed far more than she had intended. Her lips quirked up into a rueful smile.

'Then clearly that's a bit of a hot button for me.'

Her quiet honesty tugged at something inside him. Louis lifted his shoulders, suddenly fighting to stay in control.

'We all have them.'

'Right.' She turned around finally, her back leaning on the glass.

Fearless. Proud.

A fracture splintered through his chest.

He told himself it was just part of the game. The better they knew each other, the closer they could appear to be for the cameras. But then her smile suddenly widened, the faintest hint of a gleam in her eye as she spoke.

'I could let you into a little secret.'

And he knew that telling himself such lies was tantamount to slapping a sticking plaster over a gaping wound and hoping it would do the job.

'What's that?'

'I wasn't always as driven or wholesome as everyone seems to think.'

It was impossible not to be swept along with her. How was it possible she could lift the mood with a single smile, a single look?

'Let me guess, you got a B in one of your medical courses,' he teased.

She actually rolled her eyes at him.

'You see? No one really gets me.'

There was no reason that should rankle as much as it did. No reason for him to take it as a challenge. To want to be the first—the only—person who she couldn't say that to.

'Go on, then.' He arched his eyebrows. 'Shock me.'

She pushed off the glass abruptly, strolling across the room to the view on the other side.

'I almost got expelled when I was fifteen. I nearly didn't even get my GCSEs, let alone my A levels.'

'You did?' He snorted. 'Sorry, no chance.'

'It's true.' He could almost believe she was enjoying this. Shocking him. 'I suddenly realised I was this teenage girl who had lost her mum and I fell into all the typical traps. I couldn't see the point of school, or learning. The doctors hadn't been able to save either her or Jack, so what was the point? I fell in with a different crowd and started ditching school, playing truant.'

'What, to go and drink cider and sit around the local park?' He was incredulous, but that only served to make her laugh all the more.

'Actually, we went to the local pool hall and spent all day in there. The brother of one of the group worked there, so if anyone ever came looking he'd let us out the emergency exit. Wow, I used to love that game.'

'And you did that for weeks? A month?'

Why did this only add to the admiration he had for her? The fact that whatever demons she'd had in the past, the intelligent, quick-thinking, professional doctor she was today only proved she'd beaten them all.

'Almost a year. My father eventually took me in hand. Told me some home truths, like what my mother would think of me if she saw me.' She raised her chin and for the first time Louis realised how fine the line was that she was treading, between laughing and crying. 'It was the first time he'd ever really talked about her to me. Before that, everything I knew, all the photos I had of her had come from my grandparents.'

'Yet you turned your life around again,' he breathed. 'Look at you now.'

'Yes, I turned it around.' She tilted her head from one side to the other in a devilish little dance. 'But not before I'd been put back an academic year. It was mortifying, but some of the others from that crowd hadn't even been given that opportunity so I knew I had to swallow it. I worked. God, I worked. I worked so hard that by the time I came to sit my GCSEs I'd already been put back into my old year group. After that I never looked back.'

'Never?' he challenged softly, her slow smile burning hotly through him as she shook her head.

'Never.'

'Then how about we do a little fun, nostalgic looking back now?'

He had no idea why he did it, but Louis held out his hand, waiting as she saw it, tried to resist it.

'What do you mean?'

'Trust me,' he prompted quietly.

'Why?' Suspicion warred with curiosity.

'Do you trust me?'

The question was so much more important than he'd intended. And her answer suddenly carried that much more weight.

Instead, Alex chose not to say a word. She lifted her eyes to his, scanning his face and searching for answers to questions she couldn't bring herself to ask. And then, just as he was about to wonder at the sense of what he'd done, she crossed the floor almost as if against her own will, and fitted her hand into his as he led her to the helical staircase in the centre of the room.

Wordlessly she kicked off her heels and jogged lightly up the stairs behind him, her fingers still laced through his and her trust in him implicit.

Something barrelled through Louis. He needed to call a halt to everything now. It suddenly felt all too intimate.

She felt too intimate.

Sex was one thing, but being emotionally close to someone? That was something he didn't want to risk.

Instead, he pulled her next to him, his arm slipping around her waist, not sure whether he was talking about the view or what was happening between them.

'Open your eyes,' he ground out brusquely.

CHAPTER SIX

ALEX STARED AT the full-size snooker table, a gurgle rumbling up from somewhere deep inside her.

'It isn't quite the quality of table I learned on.' She grinned. 'But I appreciate the nostalgia.'

Louis laughed. 'It isn't quite the quality I learned on either. I was taught by Arnaud, our estate hand—though he's now the estate manager. They had a beat-up pool table in one of the old stable blocks. My grandfather used to sneak in there a few times and he and I would have a game. When he died, Arnaud was the closest thing to a father figure I had left.'

'Is the table still there?'

'I doubt it. But the stable blocks are mine, maybe I'll renovate them one of these days. There's a covenant to say I can use them for any activity, providing it's legal and doesn't damage the estate.'

'You want a game?' she asked quickly.

'Why not? Snooker, billiards or pool?'

'You choose.'

It was daft and fun and none of the ways she would ever have imagined her evening with Louis ending up. No doubt he would say the same thing.

It was amazing how the time disappeared after that. Lost in a haze of happier childhood memories—at least, comparatively—and the unexpected discoveries that they loved many of the same books and bands, shared some similar interests and wanted to travel to similar destinations. Even politics wasn't off limits and they marvelled at their similar opinions and indulged in a couple of lively debates where they did differ. They laughed, drank wine and talked, even finding an old action film they both remembered, which spawned yet more nostalgic memories.

Her only real moment of envy came when he told her he'd visited Machu Picchu on a trek with his grandfather, while she knew she would probably never get that opportunity. When she remembered how their lives had differed. Still differed now.

It was the kind of first date she could only have dreamed of in the real world. The fact that it had happened so organically, so unexpectedly, with Louis—on a first date that hadn't even been real—made it both inspiring and aggravating at the same time.

'You're a revelation,' he told her abruptly, stopping as they passed one another around the table, allowing his hand to cup her cheek.

And all she could do was stand still and let him, afraid to move lest she break the spell. Her insides turned molten, not least when he dragged his thumb across her lower lip.

'Why don't you act like this in public, Louis?' The question slipped out before she could stop it. 'Why always the playboy act?'

'Who says it's an act?'

She might have thought regret shadowed his eyes, but that couldn't be right.

'I do. I don't think you enjoy it any more, if you ever really did. But I can't help but wonder if it's how you protect yourself from forming relationships. Because you're afraid you'll lose someone else the way you did your mother.'

Louis hadn't banked on the way she seemed to creep into his head without him even noticing her advance. The way that when she looked at him, the expression in her ice-blue eyes was hot enough to melt entire glaciers, speaking to his very sex.

He should shut her down, but he couldn't quite manage it. Time to turn the tables instead.

'I can think of a lot more interesting pastimes than a sixty-second pop psychology session,' he countered suggestively.

'You do see that you use sex as a distraction when the conversation heads off into waters you don't like?' she demanded.

Her voice was a little too husky. Still, it hadn't escaped him that she had a point.

'You credit me with too much guile.' He summoned a practised grin and stepped closer to her. 'Maybe I just enjoy sex. Pure, unadulterated, animal sex.'

She held her ground but he didn't miss the way her pulse jumped at her throat. Did that pretty flush currently sweeping over her pretty face also extend to that indecently sexy body of hers? How he'd love to find out.

'Stop it.'

A half-hearted mutter at best. He let his hand skim over her jawline and her breathing grew shallower, the swell of her soft breasts visible with each inhalation. His palms actually ached to touch her, to discover whether her nipples were as taut, as perfect as they'd felt against his chest a few hours before.

'Why? You can't deny there's an attraction between us. We both felt it even at the gala, and if there was any doubt then that kiss back at the restaurant dispelled it.'

He took another step, his hands restrained in his pockets, letting her be the one to reach out and make contact, palms flat against his chest but by no means pushing him away.

'Fine.' A gurgle of triumph rumbled in his body at the vaguely strangled sound. 'There's an attraction there, I can't deny it. But, apparently unlike you, I can control myself without having to pursue every desire that takes hold of me.'

'Do you pursue any?' he demanded, and she gave a quiet gasp.

'Are you calling me frigid?'

'I wasn't.' His tone was even, unconcerned. 'But I find it interesting that *you* should choose the term. Is it something you've been accused of in the past?'

She lifted her head defiantly.

'No. It is not.'

'Ah.' Louis nodded gently. 'Then it's merely your own hang-up.'

'You...don't know what you're talking about.'

The moment of hesitation said it all. A heavy silence swirled around them for a moment until Louis chose to take pity on her.

Or himself.

There was no room for the sentimental side of Louis Delaroche. It wasn't what people wanted to see. It wasn't what he wanted to see. And he didn't appreciate the way Alex kept excavating little memories that he'd long-since buried.

He'd rather go back to the arrogant playboy Louis than be the man who still wondered at what might have been.

As if sensing him closing off to her, Alex tugged herself free and backed away. This time he didn't try to stop her. She seemed to get under his skin both mentally and physically.

His lips still burned with the memory of their kiss. The ghost of it still lingered, haunting him with its feigned promise. *Rattling* him, when nothing ever got to him. Making him feel out of control, vulnerable.

The thought pulled him up sharply. He wouldn't allow himself to be vulnerable. Emotions were for those too weak to control themselves. Surgery gave him the only buzz, the only kick, the only sense of triumph and pride that he needed. Especially when he carried out intricate, hail-Mary procedures that lesser surgeons shied away from even when they had nothing left to lose.

He might need to tame his wild, arrogant playboy reputation in order to finally start to wrest the Delaroche Foundation from the hands of the self-serving Jean-Baptiste, but that didn't mean he had to change who he was under the surface.

Since when had he allowed himself to become confused over just how fake his relationship with Alex really was?

How had she slipped under his skin?

What he felt when he was around her was lust, pure and simple. Surely he should know that better than most?

It was merely the circumstances of their meeting, Alex's fierce drive to save Rainbow House coupled with the fact they were both struggling with the loss of a parent who had loved them, only to be left with a parent who had never wanted them, was confusing the issue. The bond they seemed to share was an illusion, nothing more. That was all there was to it. The sooner he recovered his infamous, flirtatious side, the better.

'I think maybe we should go to bed,' she cut into his thoughts, offering him the perfect recovery.

Alex realised too late the suggestive nature of her comment.

'Is that so?'

His lazy drawl might have been the most sensual sound she'd ever heard in her life. It certainly shot through her to her very core.

'Alone, I mean. Not to the same bed.' She sounded ridiculously flustered. 'That is… Oh, it sounded far less suggestive in my head.'

But instead of teasing her a little more, as she'd expected, Louis simply placed a hand on her arm, apparently oblivious to the jolt of electricity that zipped from her shoulder to her fingertips.

'Relax, Alexandra, I know what you meant. Come on, I'll show you to your suite.'

'My…suite?'

'You would prefer to sleep in my suite?'

She shook her head even though, leading the way back down the incredible staircase, he couldn't see her.

'Of course not. I just assumed…well, I thought… the couch.'

She was sounding more and more like a stumbling, naïve fool as the moments wore on, she realised in dismay.

'I suppose you could sleep on the couch if you prefer, but I can assure you that the bedroom is decidedly more comfortable.'

'You know that isn't what I meant.'

He didn't acknowledge that. But, then again, he didn't refute it either. Alex wrinkled her nose as she hastily snatched up her discarded footwear, which to her eye painted an intimate, if inaccurate, scene, and followed him back into the rather grand hallway, where he was collecting her small case, and through a double archway she hadn't spotted upon her arrival.

'Your suite is this way.' Louis headed up the corridor, stopping, in a rather gentlemanly way, at the double doors and putting her bag down, as if whatever lay beyond was to be, at least for the time being, her private sanctum in which she could feel secure. 'Through there you have a bedroom, bathroom and sitting area. Should you want me for anything, I'll be in the master suite down that way.'

Alex turned obligingly as he indicated the opposite end of a corridor, which was probably the same length as her entire back garden. Possibly longer. It was difficult not to feel intimidated and only reminded her that, if this hadn't been a charade, such a coupling could never have worked.

'See you in the morning.'

The words seemed to pulse in the air. As Louis turned and walked away, a thousand different responses flew around Alex's head until, in the end, she plumped for one.

'Yes. See you in the morning.'

But he had already turned back into the main living area and out of sight. And even when she closed the door to her suite, she stayed against the door for a long time, remembering his touch and his taste and craving more.

CHAPTER SEVEN

A LOW, UNFAMILIAR sound jarred Alex out of slumber the following morning. Not that she had any idea how she'd managed to fall asleep, plagued as she had been by visions of Louis, and by erotic memories of his mouth claiming hers over and over again.

Even now her body burned with all the things she'd wanted him to do. Although the ridiculous winceyette nightgown she'd chosen to wear—the one she'd been sent as a Christmas gift years ago and had never once even considered wearing—wasn't helping. She almost hadn't packed it, hadn't lifted it out of the dusty package from the top corner of her wardrobe when she'd been racing around her home the previous night. But then she'd thought of Louis, and how weak her resolve seemed around him, and she'd decided to make a point to herself by bringing it along.

Was she really being foolish, denying herself the night with Louis that she so obviously wanted, simply because of fear? Or was her refusal to indulge such a base urge a logical, well-considered matter of self-preservation?

Alex couldn't be sure. All she knew was that she'd wrestled with the dilemma until the small hours, and now she was exhausted with her brain apparently unable to process what had woken her. She squeezed her eyes shut, her ears straining that little bit harder.

Wait? A vacuum cleaner?

She swivelled her head, which felt as though someone had exchanged it for a wrecking ball, and peered at the clock. What confused her most? The early hour or the notion of Louis vacuuming?

Common sense finally made an appearance. Scurrying out of bed and through her suite, she opened the door the tiniest crack and peered out. Of course it wouldn't be him out there.

Louis was the kind of man to employ a cleaner. And someone to do his dry-cleaning. And someone to take his dry-cleaning away in the first instance. Basically, Louis had *people.* But *people* could not catch her sleeping in the guest suite at least fifteen metres down the hall from Louis's suite. Alex squinted, praying for someone to step into view yet dreading the idea that they would. The sound appeared to be coming from the hallway off the corridor, but she couldn't see anything. She leaned back on the wall, her mind racing as she tried to figure out what to do next.

Why wasn't Louis out there, stopping them? Funny, but she wouldn't have taken him for a heavy sleeper.

Reaching into the closet, her hand only hovering for a moment, Alex slipped the previously unused dressing gown off the hanger she'd placed it on the previous night, slipped her phone into her pocket, and prised the door open again.

There was still no sign of movement, but she would have to pass the archway to get from her suite to Louis's master suite. It was, as they said, now or never.

Scuttling down the hallway as quietly as she could—it only occurred to Alex that the sound of the vacuum would have masked her footsteps by the time she reached the archway—she paused to peek around the corner. The unmistakeable figure of a woman clad in a tunic, black trousers and sensible shoes vigorously working a machine confirmed Alex's fears and sent her heart bouncing violently up into the region of her oesophagus.

With a final dash across the door opening, Alex

hurried to the end of corridor, and after her first tentative knock went unanswered, she let herself in before the cleaner rounded the corner and spotted her. With relief, she noted the suite was a mirror image of hers, although the décor was a little more masculine, the sofas more Louis-style, the elegant, darker wood of the furniture giving the impression that the room was naturally Louis's, rather than having been carefully selected by some designer with a brief. Her eyes were drawn involuntarily to a broad antique-looking desk. Beautiful, unmistakable workmanship, a piece of furniture that she might have even chosen for herself.

Her stomach twisted and flopped. It was getting harder and harder to reconcile the fast lifestyle, typical bad-boy Louis with the sophisticated, complex man she was getting to know. But she shouldn't be here, it was very much Louis's personal space. And she was invading it.

In two minds, Alex hovered where she was. Then she edged back to the door that led back into the hallway and nervously wrapped her fingers around the door handle, wondering if she should leave. She inched the door open, only for the sound of the vacuum to assail her again.

No, leaving was definitely not an option.

Alex scrambled back across the room and pressed her hands to the set of doors on the other side, which could only lead through to the bedroom, and rapped softly, her voice little more than a whisper.

'Louis?'

Silence.

She rapped again, sharper this time, but there was still no response.

Her pulse beat wildly at her wrists, making her arms almost tingle with anticipation. As if she'd run a marathon when all she'd done was manage a brief hallway sprint. But it wasn't about the distance, it was about her proximity to Louis's bedroom right this moment; the fact that entering the room where he slept, where his bed was, seemed so utterly personal.

For the first time in years, Alex dithered. Then the sound of the vacuum grew suddenly louder and she knew the cleaner must have rounded the corner into the corridor. Time was running out.

Pulling her lips into a grim line, Alex sucked in a deep breath, placed her palm on the door handle and pushed. The door offered no resistance at all, swinging easily despite its obvious solid weight, and silently inviting her into the room beyond. It took her everything she had to step through.

Light danced playfully off every surface, startling and disorientating her, but there was no mistaking the source. A bank of glass lined one side of the bedroom, but rather than giving out to the city view, as in the other rooms of the apartment, inviting blue waters lay on the other side of this windowed wall. For a moment she thought she was peering into an aquarium with no sea life in sight, although something had to have been in there recently as it was these agitated waters that were catching the light and bouncing the reflections back into the bedroom.

Louis's bedroom.

For a moment she'd almost forgotten. Yet now she looked around it was hard to believe she'd missed the oversized bed on the other side of the room, which looked as though it had been hewn from the oldest, strongest, most striking of English oaks.

It was also *unmade.*

Alex swallowed. Hard.

Crisp, white sheets had been thrown off and there was a single dent on a plump Oxford-pillowcased pillow. Her mind accelerated away from her, dragging her along as though she were tied to them with ropes. Louis, naked, in those sheets. Had his mind tossed and turned last night with images of her, the way hers had of him?

Probably not. That shame was no doubt hers alone. At least he wasn't here to witness her bursting in on him. *But where* was *he?*

Abruptly a movement at around ceiling level snagged her attention and she whirled round to catch a figure diving into the water that she now realised was a swimming pool. Louis was cutting through the water, fast and skilful, his front crawl one of which even a world-class athlete would be proud.

Did the man have to excel at everything?

He was spellbinding. Hard, unyielding lines, breathtakingly masculine.

A low ache made itself felt between her legs. The same low ache she'd been pretending she didn't feel all night. The same way she'd pretended she didn't recall exactly how his hypnotising physique felt against her body.

But she'd only been fooling herself. She remembered it all. How he'd felt. How he'd tasted. How he hadn't simply kissed her but had claimed her. Somehow branded her. Here, now, in his bedroom and looking at him through the glass wall, she couldn't fool herself any longer. It was time to abandon the notion that she could somehow control the spark that darted and sizzled between them. Somehow master it. She could no more command the attraction they shared than she could save a terminally ill patient, although her analogy felt just as deadly.

It was as if the more she tried to deny her attraction to Louis, the greater his hold over her became. He demonstrated a determination, a drive, a competitive edge in every facet of his life, even right here in the privacy of his own pool. Characteristics Alex had always found to be utterly compelling, but never more so than in the utterly focussed Louis.

And more and more she was moving away from the idea this mad scheme with Louis was a hail Mary to save Rainbow House for now, and towards the consideration that Louis might be her best chance ever for securing the future of the place for a very long time in the future.

Somewhere along the line she'd gone from suspecting his motives to trusting more than she'd trusted anyone in a very, very long while.

When had that happened?

As if sensing her thoughts, Louis turned his head, his gaze slamming without warning into hers, and she felt pinned to the spot with the intensity of it. Her whole body came alive when he stared at her that way. As though he saw nothing else but her.

She had no idea how long they stayed that way. It could have been seconds, or even a minute—she had no doubts that Louis was some kind of Poseidon, able to hold his breath for just as long as he desired under that water. She watched, riveted, as he kicked out, propelling himself up to the surface and to the edge, where he pulled himself out of the water with apparent ease.

And then he was gone and still she stood there, staring into the roughly churning water and wondering why she suddenly felt so lost. She started towards the glass wall, her nose almost pressed to it as she looked up to the water's surface.

'Something wrong?'

Alex spun around, her tongue apparently glued to the roof of her mouth.

'Alex, is everything all right?' Louis demanded, descending a set of stairs in the bedroom that had been concealed like an illusion against the panelled wall behind it. Just as the layout of the room had concealed the fact that there was a mezzanine level at all.

But it wasn't the clever architecture that had humiliatingly stolen her voice. Bare chested and glistening with beaded water, a towel now wrapped around his waist, Louis's presence filled the space, making it feel too small to contain him, pressing in on her and leaving her unable to even draw a breath.

She opened her mouth to speak but nothing came out. Louis's mouth curled up in almost grim triumph.

'Or perhaps you were just missing me after all?'

The wryness in his tone licked through her like flames racing over a wood-dust floor, and in its potency it created a smoke fog in her head, smothering all but the most inappropriate, indecent thoughts. She tried to snag her eyes from the tiniest of rivers making their way down the contours of the muscular V of his body but found that she couldn't. Her fingers itched to follow the path of the water, to trace their route, to smooth their flow, to actually *lick* them away.

Ludicrous.

And still she couldn't shake the image. Couldn't seem to regain control of her senses. She went first hot, then cold, and then impossibly hot again. And all the while Louis kept on approaching her, closing the space between them tantalisingly slowly. She needed to move, back away, turn to the side, do *anything* to halt his advance. It took her all her time to swallow. Hard.

'Though if it were the latter I'd have expected something a little…*less* than whatever it is you're wearing right now.'

That damned winceyette nightie. His grin was as wicked as if he could read her mind. It shouldn't have been possible to make the situation any worse and yet as Alex flushed and her hands clutched at her chest to pull the material together—unnecessary since it already might as well have been a tent over her entire body—she realised she couldn't have done a better job of broadcasting her lust if she'd hired a big screen in the car park of the hospital itself.

'Where did you get it from?' he continued, his rakish grin scraping through her, raw and exhilarating. 'Your ninety-year-old grandmother's wardrobe?'

'Very funny.'

To her chagrin she could hear the huskiness in her voice. Louis's eyes glinted but, try as she may, she couldn't seem to loosen her grip. If anything, she found herself gripping the fabric even tighter. Still he didn't slow his advance and Alex was forced to crane her neck up to watch him.

They both knew it was a deliberate ploy on his part.

'Is this your idea of seductive nightwear?'

'This is my idea of never becoming another notch on Louis Delaroche's bedpost nightwear,' she muttered, wishing her traitorous body had also bought into such a notion.

'Ah, I see.' Reaching her, he stepped right into her personal space and placed his hands on her shoulders, as if testing her.

Pull away, her head screamed. Her body—with the mental equivalent of sticking its fingers in its ears—refused to move a millimetre.

'Is it working?' he enquired over-politely, as if he was unaware of the current flowing between them, his touch like an flash on her skin.

Alex wavered. There was something she had to tell him. A reason she was here. For a brief second it was there, on the periphery of her mind, and she mentally lunged for it, but then Louis let one hand slide off her shoulder, his fingers brushing over the cotton, his touch scorching her flesh underneath, and for the life of her she couldn't remember anything any more.

'Is this really what you slept in?'

Her cheeks flushed, she could feel the heat. As if he knew she'd hated every second of the unfamiliar, rough material when she could have been wearing a lot less and revelling in the high thread count of Louis's luxurious sheets.

'Where did you get it from?' he pressed, his amusement refusing to abate.

Much like her embarrassment.

'My great-aunt sent it to me when I bought my first home. She thought I might get…cold.'

'She didn't think that, as a doctor, you could probably afford a place that had its own heating?' He arched an eyebrow.

It was a battle just to unstick her tongue from the roof of her mouth. It felt as though she'd just swallowed a spoonful of peanut butter.

'She remembered her first home. She had coal fires but no central heating. She's quite old, ninety-six. But still going strong. Anyway, I guess you weren't too far off the mark with your first observation about it looking as though it was something I'd got from my ninety-year-old grandmother's wardrobe.'

She was babbling. It was as much a giveaway as anything.

'Is that so?' True to form, Louis was tracing his fingertips across the material over her collarbone and she couldn't help but shiver. The corners of his mouth turned up ever so slightly. 'It's in remarkably pristine condition. One might almost believe you'd never worn it before.'

'Well, I have,' she lied, shame rippling through her at just how easily he seemed to see through her.

'When?' The challenge was stamped on every quirk of his too-perfect face.

Alex gritted her teeth.

'Lots of times.'

'Is that so? Because it looks almost as if you wore it just for me,' he continued softly, taking another step closer so that the breath caught in her throat, her body completely forgetting how to breathe. 'Tell me, Alex, who were you trying to remind to keep their distance? Me? Or you?'

She couldn't answer. She didn't dare. Whatever she said, she'd surely give herself away. His eyes bored into hers and for the longest time she couldn't drag her gaze away, couldn't deflect him. His fingers still traced a pattern on her skin, making her whole body tighten. She craved him in a way she'd never known possible.

'Does it matter who I wore it for?' she managed. 'The fact is that I'm trying to make a point.'

'That's what I thought,' Louis muttered gruffly, his hand moving quickly to cradle the back of her head as he tugged her to him. 'You realise you wouldn't have to make a point if you weren't fighting your instinct, of course?'

It was a rhetorical question, which was good since she couldn't seem to make her voice work. Her blood thundered through her and, so help her, she angled her head in tacit invitation.

'I thought it would…put you off.'

'I hate to tell you,' he continued in a voice that sounded anything other than displeased, 'but it isn't working. If anything, my imagination is filling in the blanks with remarkable enthusiasm.'

'Is that supposed to be a compliment?' Her voice shook. Something still pressed in on her mind but she couldn't locate it, couldn't remember what was so urgent other than Louis, right here, right now.

'More a statement of fact.'

The low purr was reminiscent of the promising hum of a highly powered supercar moments before it roared into action and burned everything else into nothing in its wake. She shivered in anticipation. Turned inside out by Louis, even though he hadn't done anything. Yet.

But she wanted him to. Oh, how she wanted him.

He dragged his thumb across her lower lip and heat bloomed in her anew.

'Kiss me.'

Deadly soft, but nonetheless an unequivocal demand.

She could have done so many things—refused him, decried him, walked away from him. Instead, she did the worst thing possible. She obeyed him.

Tipping her head back, she arched against him, rising just slightly onto her toes, and closed the gap between them, a thousand fireworks exploding in her head, her chest, and lower, as she finally pressed her lips to his.

CHAPTER EIGHT

IT WAS NOTHING Louis had ever known before.

The moment her hot, slick mouth fitted to his, an urgent need clawed within him. Even more raw and desperate than it had been back out there, in front of the restaurant.

Because this time there was no audience. This time they couldn't pretend it was all about the game. This time there was nothing to stop them.

He deepened the kiss and the fact that Alex was lost, barely able to keep her grip on him in an effort to keep herself upright, only intensified the moment. From the delicious drugging draw of her fingernails over his muscled shoulder blades to the feel of her hair slipping through his hands like the finest silk.

His tongue slid deliciously over hers and she let out a sound that made everything tighten, coil in his lower abdomen. He cradled her cheek as though she was as precious as the irreplaceable, valuable sculptures dotted around his penthouse. And she cast every one of them into the shade.

It was bliss to kiss her. He paid homage to her lips, the corners of her mouth and then her jawline, blazing a trail of hot kisses down the neck and exulting in the way her whole body quivered in response.

When she moved against him again, moulding herself to his chest and pressing her breasts against him, he wanted her with a ferocity he hadn't known before. Up against the panelled wall, in his bed, anywhere. Everywhere.

Every way.

He wanted to feel her without the barrier of the stupid winceyette nightgown, but he could use it to his advantage. He could make her wish she'd never brought the damned thing. Spanning her ribcage with his hands, he moved his palms to circle her and flicked his thumbs over nipples straining even beneath the heavy material. She swayed instinctively against him again, a muted cry slipping from her mouth—and a curse—and triumph stabbed through him.

'Regretting your choice of night attire yet?' he murmured against her throat, feeling her pulse fluttering wildly beneath his lips.

'Shut up and take it off,' she moaned hoarsely, and he smirked all the wider.

'Soon. There's no rush, we can take our time.'

Her eyes flew open. One minute heavy-lidded and dark, the next squinting at him and taking in his grin. A low gasp escaped her.

'You're enjoying this. Teasing me.'

'Of course. Like I said, there's no rush.'

'You say it as though you're perfectly in control,' she muttered. 'Only I know you're not.'

Carefully, deliberately she moved her hips, rocking against him until she felt the unmistakeable ridge of his arousal. Solid, insistent, almost painfully hard. He hadn't such an ache, such a desperate throb in a long time. Suddenly her hands moved to the twist of his towel, which still hung low on his hips, tugging the knot and releasing it before he could react. And then she was touching him, her fingers gliding up and down his length and sending him wild with desire.

Louis groaned. Things were moving fast. Too fast. This wasn't the way he did things. He was never so…desperate. He had to slow it down, get back in control of this runaway train of need. He grasped her wrist, encircling it with his finger and thumb, and moved it from him. She protested even more when he moved her entire body from his, ignoring the way the loss of contact made him feel abruptly lost. Bereft.

Then he lifted the ugly, tent-like nightgown over her head in one easy movement, balled it up and tossed it across the room. And finally she was standing before him in nothing but the tiniest, sexiest scrap of lace he thought he'd ever seen.

'Exquisite,' he commented thickly, his hand sweeping over her shoulder, down over her chest, one perfect breast, and skimming over her abdomen before running a finger over the thin velvet band of her underwear. He traced patterns over her lower stomach and dipped low enough to brush against her hot, feminine heat, revelling in her gasp, then back up over her torso, leaving her aching for so much more.

'It's peacock-blue,' she blurted out abruptly. Rattled.

That she was so responsive to him, so brimming with need only made him all the harder. She poured through all his senses. A strange kind of insanity ran through his blood. He was consumed by her.

'I wasn't talking about the underwear,' he managed gruffly, 'so much as the woman wearing it.'

'Oh.'

So demure, so modest, so unaware of her own sexuality. *So his.*

His lips curled upwards slightly. Such a possessive sensation should have alarmed him. It didn't. Instead, he simply lowered his head and kissed her again, and she drank him in as if she thought this was her one and only chance.

It was like the most delectable adventure, kissing and nibbling and licking his way from her eager mouth, along that pretty jawline and down the long line of her elegant neck. He dawdled and dipped into the sensitive hollow that made her tremble so sublimely in his arms. When he rolled one glorious nipple in his fingers before bending his head to suck on it, his tongue swirling a pattern of its own, she called out as her fingers bit into his shoulders, her back curving as though she offered herself up to him all the more.

'I can't get enough of you,' he mumbled as he moved to lavish the same attention on her other breast.

She choked something out, but it was almost incoherent to him, and he couldn't bring himself to stop long enough to ask her to repeat it.

His hands glided over her body, acquainting

himself with every contour, every feature. Imprinting them into his head. Maybe into his very soul.

Every now and then he allowed his fingers to dip lower, but never for long. And never where she wanted him most, if her soft moans and body rolls were anything to go by. But Louis suddenly found he had his own battle to win. He wanted to make this first time last, to make it perfect for her, but his own body—up until now always well within his expert command—was threatening to spin out of his control. Every time she arched her body into him, brushing against his sex in a silent plea, he had to fight the carnal urge to pick her up, throw her on the bed and bury himself inside her until she was crying out his name and neither of them knew where each of them ended and the other began.

Almost feverish with lust, Louis dipped his head again, his teeth grazing the hollow of her neck with just enough pressure to make her gasp. To make her hips rock against him in another silent plea.

'Tell me you want me,' he commanded, the faintly salty taste of her skin teasing the end of his tongue. But he forced himself to stop, to put a gossamer-fine layer of air between them.

She could barely answer.

'What are you doing?'

She twisted to get back into his arms. He held her away.

'Say the words,' he rasped, pausing but not lifting his head.

He was reckless, and abraded, and pounding.

'I want you,' she managed to choke out. Then, as if she felt bolder, the assertion came again. More confident this time. 'I *want* you.'

'Where?'

A crimson stain spread over her lovely cheeks.

'You know where.'

'Tell me,' he ordered.

He needed there to be no doubt, no ambiguity. He knew what she thought of his morals to date. He had to hear her say what she wanted. For her to know she'd said it.

Shakily, she took hold of his wrist; moved his hand to the heat at the top of her legs, her whisper so quiet he had to strain to hear it.

'Here.'

'Here?' he enquired casually, as though it wasn't killing him to restrain himself.

She bit her lip, a jerk of a nod.

'There.'

'Better.' He didn't even try to disguise the naked need in his voice.

But it didn't matter. He had what he needed.

He nudged her over to sit on the edge of the bed. Dropping to his knees in front of her, his hand lifting one of her legs over his shoulder, Louis hooked the flimsy scrap of lace aside and pressed his mouth to the centre of her hot, honeyed need, drinking her in at last.

Alex heard herself cry out. A low, husky sound, and then nothing. She couldn't. She could barely even catch her breath.

Every single nerve in her body reacted as he licked into her core where she'd felt heavy, *so heavy*; yearning for him with a need that was almost crippling.

He muttered in French, but Alex didn't need to understand the words to know it was fierce, thick with desire. For the first time she felt desirable and wanton. Just as provocative, as sexual as the women he usually dated. Except that she wasn't, and she wasn't sure if there was something she should be doing for him. If there was something important she was forgetting.

'Louis…' She lifted herself slightly onto one elbow and tried to shift away from him for a moment.

Louis lifted his head a fraction until his smouldering gaze met hers.

'Relax,' he murmured, his breath the most sensual whisper against the softest heights of her thigh, making her all the more molten inside. 'I want to taste you. Claim you.'

He slid his hand under one leg, lifting it slightly as he shouldered his way under it, granting himself better access, and he lowered his head again, the way his eyes still locked with hers only making it all the more erotic. And then he licked into her again and it was like an explosion of fireworks across Alex's eyes.

Louis toyed with her, kissed her, sucked on her, his dexterous fingers and devious mouth working in harmony to render her completely incapable of any action. Any thought. Blood roared in her ears and she could feel his hair through the fingers she couldn't recall lacing against his head. She gave herself up to sensations she had never felt in her life before. Surely never would again.

She could feel fire inside her growing as he stoked it. Higher and higher. His long fingers slipped in and out of her even as her hips bucked involuntarily against his sinful mouth. Wild need coursed through her, dizzying, searing, clearing her mind of that last, insistent thought. He was moving faster now, making her clasp at the luxurious bedsheets in a hopeless attempt to gain traction, her gasps and pants fast and shallow.

And then he twisted his wrist and Alex stiffened and shuddered and then simply fractured. She splintered into a thousand perfect shards. She cried out his name again and again. Still he didn't stop. Kissing her, holding her, playing with her, until she finally, *finally* stilled.

For several perfect moments Alex could almost imagine it was the start of something new. Then, abruptly, the outside doors to the suite banged, the sound of the vacuum invading her ears, and as Louis's grip loosened for a single instant, Alex rolled back on the bed, exhaling in dismay. But not for what she'd let Louis do, instead simply for the fact that they'd been interrupted.

That was what she'd forgotten.

'Your cleaning lady,' she breathed heavily.

'That's what woke me up this morning. That's why I'm here.'

His low curse reverberated between them and he crossed the room in two long strides. They were lucky the woman was still in the sitting area on the other side of the bedroom doors.

'Wait here,' he barked out. 'She can't see you like this.'

'That was what I thought…' Alex blurted after him.

But he was already gone, leaving her alone in the middle of his bedroom. And the shivers that accompanied her were nothing whatsoever to do with the temperature.

What had she been thinking? Losing herself with Louis to the extent that she'd even forgotten someone could walk in on them at any moment. That wasn't who she was. It wasn't who she'd ever been.

But it was who playboy Louis was.

It was one thing to agree to this charade of a relationship, the engagement to come and ultimately the marriage. To pretend she could be bought as a wife. It was quite another to actually *act* as though she was some booty call mistress.

The worst thing about it was that a part of her

didn't want to listen. A part of her wanted to wait for Louis to come back through those doors and pick back up with her exactly where he'd left off.

Hot shame flooded through her.

Scampering off the bed, she searched the room for the nightgown that he'd balled up and tossed. It wasn't hard to spot, lying on the floor on the other side of the bed like some huge, cheap rug.

Mocking her.

She hurried over and snatched it up, tussling with the long, ruffled sleeves, which had been pulled inside out in the moment, pretending she didn't see the buttons that he'd torn off in his haste.

Righting it, she tugged it back over her head, telling herself she was glad it was as frumpy and unflattering as it was, and moved to the doors to listen.

She could hear the tone of the conversation, as one-way as it was, even if the words themselves were too muffled to get the detail. Still, she could tell that Louis was brief, firm, yet nonetheless polite; was forced to admit that it was a world away from the arrogant, entitled man who the press loved to hate.

Then he was closing the door as he stepped back

into the room. Just the two of them, again. Him in his towel, her in her nightgown, just as they'd been at the start of this thing. Still, this time he kept his distance, staying across the floor from her.

She didn't know whether to feel relieved or hurt. She only knew that the air felt thick around them. Oppressive. And she didn't know what that meant.

'She's leaving,' Louis stated flatly, but somehow she didn't get the impression that he just meant the bedroom corridor.

Alex shook her head. Why did everything feel so muggy?

'Who's leaving?'

Louis offered a clipped nod.

'Janelle, my cleaning lady. For the day. Just give her a few minutes.'

'You can't be expecting to just pick up where you left off,' she accused, guilt lending her voice a harsher quality.

'You want to pretend you don't want that?' He raised an eyebrow, faintly mocking her.

'I'm not pretending anything.'

'So you admit you want me.'

She swallowed.

'I don't want you.'

'Is this the game we're back to playing?' he

asked quietly, dangerously, enough to make her skin prickle in warning. 'Because I can tell you now, Alex, that I'm bored with it.'

'We agreed this was a business arrangement. A marriage in name only. We agreed there would be no sex.'

If only her body wasn't protesting every word she was saying.

'We didn't agree anything of the sort,' Louis stated calmly. 'It was never discussed.'

'Because it went without saying.'

'No, because I always assumed somewhere down the line you'd give up your ridiculous notion of pretending this intense attraction between us didn't exist.'

'So you always planned to seduce me.' She crossed her arms disdainfully.

'I was always expecting this moment to arise. I was always waiting for you to tell me you wanted me. And exactly *where* you wanted me,' he countered, the deliberate emphasis causing another blush to colour her cheeks.

'That's why you made me say it.'

'I just wanted to hear it,' he said softly. 'And I intend to hear it again and again in the weeks and months to come.'

'You won't,' she bit out. 'Because this will never happen again. Nothing like this can ever happen between us again.'

'That's where you're wrong, *amour.*' His calm tone was almost worse than if he'd been angry. 'Because now that I know just how much you want me, now that I have irrefutable proof of how incredible we would be together, I have no intention of this marriage being merely a charade.'

'You can't make me…'

'Of course not,' he scorned. 'Neither would I ever dream of it. But I would never have to. You will come to me.'

'No, I most certainly won't.' Was her thudding heart because of her conviction, or because she was terribly afraid that he was right?

'You will,' he assured her, his wicked smile going right to her core, where she was still soft, still wet from his masterful play. 'Just like you did this morning.'

She couldn't seem to stop her teeth from worrying at her lip. As long as they were in such close proximity there was a good chance she would once again give in to the baser needs that Louis seemed to have unearthed in her.

She tipped her head back, barely stopping herself from rising up onto her toes.

'Then it's lucky you're working away in France for the next month or so.'

As victories went, it didn't feel like much of one. Rather, she felt empty at the prospect.

'Luckier still that you're coming with me.'

She told herself that her heart didn't leap. His unwavering gaze didn't help matters.

'I can't. I have work.'

'You can and you have to. I'll deal with the hospital. If we're to convince the press we're together, that this engagement is a true whirlwind romance and not a sham, then you have no choice. That's if you want me to claim control of the Lefebvre Group and save Rainbow House, of course. What is more important to you? This false sense of pride or Rainbow House?'

He had her. They both knew it. She still quashed the part of her that rejoiced at the knowledge.

'Then this nonsensical exchange is over?'

She opened her mouth to object but knew she couldn't. His wry smile still turned her on.

'Good. So, we shall be staying at Chateau Rochepont—'

'Your family estate?' she cut in. 'The press will

have a field day. You've never taken any woman back there.'

Her body felt compressed, tight, too small for her skin. It was only intensified by his inscrutable expression.

Had this always been part of the plan? Or had it developed in the last few minutes?

'All the more reason to make a point of it now, don't you think?'

'I can't—'

'It's non-negotiable.'

He was back to his Louis voice. Imperious, inflexible. Part of her didn't even care. He wanted her with him. Nevertheless, she shook her head.

'Louis, I can't… I need more time… I…'

'The point of you moving in here was to be with me so that I could help you avoid the media after last night at the restaurant. If I'm not around, who will protect you?'

'I can look after myself,' she argued. 'Besides, surely the very fact that you have all this security to get up here makes it safer than my little house. I still have to go to the hospital, carry out my work.'

'They can replace you.'

'I owe it to Gordon to give him time to choose

a replacement.' She knew that would halt him. Louis respected her mentor as much as she did. She pressed her advantage. 'A *temporary* replacement.'

'Fine. I'll give you three days. But don't say I didn't warn you that the press would hound you. I'll trust you not to let them rattle you.'

'Louis—'

'Three days, Alex, and then you *will* join me out there,' he said, shutting her down. 'It will be the perfect setting for a public proposal to cement our plan.'

Her throat was suddenly painfully dry.

'The plan.' She wasn't sure how she managed to nod, let alone speak. 'Right.'

'And, Alex…' His voice rasped, pushing down the feeble defences she was frantically trying to reinstate. 'We will be revisiting what happened here this morning. I can promise you that much.'

She told herself that the gurgling sensation was her stomach roiling at Louis's highhandedness, and not a bubbling excitement at being alone with him for the next month or so.

She almost believed it, too.

CHAPTER NINE

'RIGHT, I NOW have your bloodwork results, your MRI and EMG. And I can say that I believe that facial decompression surgery is a good treatment option in your case, since there isn't any damage to the facial nerve itself.'

He smiled gently as his patient and her partner promptly dissolved into tears of joy. The paralysis that had left one half of her face severely drooped had affected her confidence and quality of life considerably and other less invasive treatments of the paralysis had been unsuccessful.

It was good to be delivering positive news, but ultimately Louis couldn't help but feel happy today for anything which would keep his mind off the fact that Alex would be arriving in less than a couple of hours. In fact, she would probably be getting ready to board the plane right about now.

It still needled him that he'd had to fight her about taking his own private jet instead of some commercial airline. That she hadn't just obeyed him. Accepted that the private plane would make her life—and flight—far more pleasant. No doubt she'd been making a point to him. But he didn't care. She had acquiesced in the end and she was coming, and the latter was what really mattered. The chemistry had been there all along but the fact that, for the first time in his life, he was resisting it had to be the reason Alexandra Vardy got under his skin in a way that no other woman ever had.

While she'd pretended to him, and to herself, that she didn't want sex, he'd kept his distance as best he could. But hearing her acknowledge that she wanted him had been pivotal. It had been the moment he'd realised that if he wanted to conquer this apparent *longing* he'd inconveniently developed for the woman, he was going to have to take every opportunity to slake this effervescing thirst for each other.

He'd told her to call it a break away, and he hadn't been entirely joking. Getting Alex away from work, from the UK, from the press, would no doubt help her to relax. Make her see that denying the attraction that thundered between them was only feeding it all the more. Once they'd slaked their physical desire they could get on with the task in hand without such unwanted complications.

He carefully ignored the voice that echoed in his head that he was being naïve, and pulled his concentration back to his patient before it could wander too far. Another thing that had never, not once, happened to him in his professional life with any other woman before.

'At this stage my plan would be to carry out a mastoidectomy, which is where I would remove part of the mastoid bone behind your ear in order that your inflamed facial nerve might have enough room to expand, thereby relieving some of the pressure that is no doubt causing some of the symptoms of your facial paralysis.'

'That's wonderful,' the woman choked out. 'I can't believe it.'

'I'm sure you already know this,' he encouraged, 'but the facial nerve, also known as the cranial nerve VII, serves many vital functions, not just the motor function that allows you to smile and frown. Although we always prefer the smiling.'

His gentle joking elicited a smile, as he'd hoped it would, keeping them positive and engaged so that he could get across as much important information as he could.

'The anticipation would be that, as well as some facial control, you should experience some degree of return of gland function in your eyes, nose and mouth, making it easier to close your eye and even to blink, so there would be less need for the eyedrops all the time; and improvements to both your senses of smell and taste.'

'And if the drooping is reduced then she'll be less prone to accidentally biting her inner cheek, right, Doc?' the patient's partner asked, and Louis couldn't help noticing the way the couple squeezed hands in a silent, supportive conversation of their own.

Though there was no logical explanation, it made him think of Alex all over again.

'It should,' he agreed. 'So fewer ulcerations and infections. But, as I said, it won't wholly reverse the paralysis. And I do need to warn you that it might take up to a year for optimal results, and there will still be a significant degree of asymmetry.'

'That's okay,' she managed, her barely contained emotion making her sound slightly more indistinct than usual. 'It's better than what I have now.'

'And how is work?' Louis asked as carefully as he could. 'Are your colleagues understanding about your condition?'

'Actually, I'm a teaching assistant specialising in children with severe learning difficulties. Some of them just asked outright, a few of them were a little unsettled in the beginning, and some of them struggle anyway with emotions and empathy. However, I'm lucky that for the most part, as long as I act the same towards them, give them the same love and care, it doesn't really matter to them how I look.'

'That's good.' He forced an understanding smile onto his face.

Even as he walked the couple to the door, his mouth still talking to them, his mind was on Alex.

Why was it that everything seemed to pull him straight back around to her? The way that, unlike his patient, it hadn't mattered what she'd done, she was never going to win her father's love. Never going to make him forgive her for not being a match for her brother. For not being the saviour sibling. Something that had never been within her control.

And yet, despite all that, she still fought so damned fiercely for Rainbow House.

How many other kids were like Alex?

Like him?

It struck him that there had to be more he could do to help. Not just Rainbow House, but places like it. For Alex. For his mother. For himself.

He might be pretending to the world that he was changing, he might even convince them all. But that was all about perceptions. Up until now he hadn't really believed he *would* change. Not deep down.

Maybe he could.

Alex seemed to believe it.

Closing the door behind the couple, Louis picked up his ringing phone, knowing exactly who it was going to be, and part of him wished he could just ignore it and will his father away.

And yet he should be celebrating. Rejoicing in the fact that if Jean-Baptiste was calling him, it was because he was beginning to panic. Because his father was being forced to recognise that support for Louis was beginning to gain momentum.

It should fill him with jubilation. Instead, it was shadowed by Louis's delight in knowing that in a matter of hours Alex would be back in his life. Tonight, he was determined, she would be back in his arms.

His father was little more than an unwelcome interruption.

'Oui?' Louis demanded curtly, clicking it onto speakerphone and sliding the phone across his desk as he busied his hands with sorting a few files.

His father's fast, angry tone barked at him in Franglais, a sure sign that he was mad.

'You're seeing *la putain* who tried to corner me at the gala *soirée*?'

Louis sucked in a deep breath. Then another.

He would not allow himself to be baited.

'I'm seeing Alexandra Vardy, a respected doctor at Silveroaks Hospital. She's Gordon's protégé,' he added with painstaking breeziness. 'I know you'd be impressed if you saw how skilled an anaesthetist she is. Oh, and I should also inform you that Alex is coming out to the estate.'

'No, she most certainly is not.'

'Too late, I'm afraid,' Louis injected with deliberate calmness. 'She's already around thirty-six thousand feet.'

The silence suggested his father was uncharacteristically apoplectic in his characteristic rage. Louis almost smiled into the silent phone, though it was a hard, brittle excuse for a smile.

'I forbid it,' Jean-Baptiste spluttered eventually.

And there again was the easily enraged man Louis knew all too well. It was gratifying to know that not everyone had been fooled by the knight-in-shining-scrubs reputation that the media had painted all these years.

'I'm not asking permission,' Louis stated in a tone so cold he could bet it would rival the Norwegian ice hotel where his father had taken his latest squeeze. 'The estate is my home, too. I'm merely taking this opportunity to inform you. Call it courtesy. This way, you don't have to engage in another disagreeable phone call to verify what will no doubt be in tomorrow's papers.'

'I know you lied to my security team to save her from the humiliation of being ejected from the ball like the unwelcome stray dog that she was. I know you play to your reputation as a playboy, Louis, but even you could have done better than scraps like that.'

Jean-Baptiste was goading him. Louis knew it. And still he clenched his fists at the barely disguised snide tone. He couldn't let the older man think he was winning. Not where Alex was concerned. Still, he had no idea how he managed it.

'Alex did mention you and she had had a little… misunderstanding that night.'

'Un malentendu?' the older man exploded, as much at Louis's calmness as at his words, but it still felt like a hollow victory. 'It was no misunderstanding. She threatened to go to the press with how the Lefebvre Group and the Delaroche Foundation are composed of one and the same board. The vitriolic little *putain* tried to claim she knew that I was transferring assets simply to sell them off and line my own pockets.'

'We both know that isn't true although, to be fair, her assumption was based on her knowledge at the time.' Louis forced himself to stay civil. He would not lose his cool. He *could* not. 'But don't worry, I've since set her straight.'

'Meaning?' The snarl rolled down the line.

'Meaning that I assured her you weren't using the Delaroche Foundation to shut down Rainbow House simply for financial gain.'

Deliberate, aimed, striking true. The silence was almost lethal.

'You told her about your mother's accident.'

'More or less.' Louis shrugged. 'They weren't my exact words.'

The gutter-level curses his father was uttering were another long-overdue, satisfying strike. Louis had a few choice names of his own he would like to throw back. But he didn't. He restrained himself, knowing Alex wouldn't approve, and it was amazing how her good opinion was suddenly driving his actions.

The cursing stopped abruptly and silence cracked instead. Air practically whistled down the phone. Icy and foreboding.

'Be very careful which side you choose to be on, Louis. Or you may find yourself dealing with questions about your mother concerning things I'm certain you would far prefer the press didn't know.'

The threat insinuated itself through the ether, filling up Louis's office until he was reaching for a window, as if the toxicity was as real as the air he was breathing.

He reached a hand up to tug at the shirt collar that suddenly seemed to have closed around his neck. He had no idea how he kept his voice as calm, as level, as he did.

'Are you threatening to tell them she committed suicide?'

'What do they say, the truth will always out?'

Emotions coursed through Louis so fast and so violent that he wasn't sure how he remained upright.

'Then perhaps it's time it did,' he managed. 'Perhaps they might ask the questions I was always too afraid of you to ask. Such as why such a strong, loyal, connected woman should be so beaten down by her husband that she felt she had no alternative than to do what she did.'

With that, Louis terminated the call. Before any of his father's poison could get to him. Before he could wonder at how, since Alex had come into his life, he suddenly had the strength to turn the tables on his father.

And that was just the start, he thought triumphantly. With her by his side, he could save Rainbow House for Alex, even if that meant temporarily claiming the birthright he'd refused to pursue all these years. The responsibility that he still didn't care to take on.

Not that it mattered. Once things had settled down he would appoint a good chairman and leave the ship in some other captain's eminently more capable control. As long as he had his surgeries. And Alex.

He couldn't stay in the room any longer. Not after that call. Snatching up his coat, Louis hurried out of the door, barely locking it behind him, and then down the stairs rather than wait for the lift.

In less than an hour Alex would be here. And he found he could scarcely wait.

Take it slowly. Don't make her bolt.

He could work the rest out from there.

Alex gazed out of the small aircraft window, trying to quell the muffled *rat-a-tat* of her heart against her chest and feeling more confused than ever.

When she'd embarked in England not ninety minutes ago, she'd been feeling a horrible combination of irritability and fragility, resenting every moment of what was to come even as the plane had climbed into the grey skies and plunged into the thick cloud cover. She'd tried to lose herself in a book, and when that hadn't worked, the latest medical journal. She'd refused the first two glasses of champagne that a silent but efficient attendant had brought to her. But at some point, right after the cloud cover had broken and warm sunshine had poured through the tiny window, she'd accepted the third attempt, stopped mumbling her speech and allowed herself to breathe for the first time in days.

Now she gazed down on the deep blue waters of the Mediterranean, glinting like jewels in the brilliant sunlight, and felt that little bit more carefree, that little less drowned in responsibility. Her champagne flute stood freshly refilled, her paperback abandoned on her lap, and her head filled with indecent images of Louis from that morning in his penthouse.

Even the memory of him made her feel alive. The anticipation of seeing him again was creating a low hum in her body that only seemed to grow louder the lower the plane descended through the French skies.

But she'd meant what she'd said when she'd told him it could never happen again.

Now, more than ever, she had to stick to her word. The last few days had been hell. Louis had warned her that the press would be unstoppable but she hadn't believed him. Instead, they'd been worse.

She turned her head to the tabloid that sat rolled up in the bag by her feet. As if *Apple Pie Alex* from her colleagues hadn't been bad enough, in the last couple of days, ever since the Louis kiss in that restaurant, the press had chosen to dub her *Vanilla Vardy.*

Vanilla Vardy too virginal for Lascivious Louis!

It might have been a compliment to her. It wasn't. It was as though even her kissing technique was plain and uninspiring and the tone all too closely matched a similar tabloid article from the other day that had breathlessly proclaimed:

Vanilla Vardy wins Luscious Louis Sympathy Vote!

As if they knew how he'd touched her that morning. She may not be a virgin per se, but it had been like she'd never been touched before, and certainly not with such an effect.

As if they knew that her response to him had been so visceral, so carnal that she'd barely even recognised herself.

She wondered if he was laughing at her the way the public would be if they'd seen the way she'd come apart so quickly in his arms. Congratulating himself on ruining her for any other man. Because he surely had.

And yet it took a real effort to bring herself to feel even a degree of remorse. To tell herself that she wasn't frustrated that they had been interrupted, or that the moment had been shattered, and that she hadn't had the courage to finish what Louis had started.

Because she'd wanted to. Oh, how she'd *ached* to. In that moment she'd known that she might never get another opportunity like that in her life, since no other man in her past had even come close to making her lose control the way she had in his bedroom. She couldn't imagine any other man in her future ever would either.

No one else would ever be able to match Louis, the way he'd made her feel, the way he'd made her writhe, the way he'd made her shatter.

There was only one Louis Delaroche.

Which was why that had to be her one and only slide into temptation. She couldn't afford to lose herself again. Couldn't afford to let him get under her skin the way he seemed to be so skilled at doing. Couldn't afford to indulge in all the fantasies she'd had over the last few nights, in which, instead of simply lying back and letting him pleasure her so thoroughly, she'd met him halfway. Doing things to him she knew she would never have the courage to try.

And that was why she had to keep her head on her shoulders from now on.

Only it wasn't that simple. Because for her, at least, there had been more than just the sex. Louis had awakened a side to her character that morning that had lain dormant for so many years that even she herself had thought it long gone. That daring, mischievous side to herself that she'd thought had died a long time ago. And she'd accepted that it was gone, almost welcomed its demise.

Who would ever have thought that Louis would be the person to resurrect it?

It didn't help that she'd received a concerned call from her father that morning to tell her that Rainbow House had been visited by a new team of hot-shot lawyers who claimed they were working on behalf of the Lefebvre Group. He'd said that they'd managed to get through a temporary injunction to stop the transfer of assets to the Delaroche Foundation. And then her father had asked, in his gruff way, if their new advocates had anything to do with Louis Delaroche and the fact that photos of her and Louis kissing had been plastered all over the papers. He'd gently warned her against doing anything that wasn't *right.* That even Rainbow House wasn't worth certain sacrifices.

And she'd lied and assured him that the two things weren't related, even as she'd swelled with happiness and something she didn't care to identify that Louis had begun to fulfil his part of the deal. That he hadn't grown bored with the venture now that he'd claimed her as his.

But that still didn't mean he was finally ready to do the right thing and take up the mantle of the Lefebvre Group, as his mother had always wanted him to do. Until he accepted that, surely it was yet another reason why she needed to separate the two, the business agreement from the sexual attraction.

It was only as the plane bumped down that Alex realised they'd landed, and the Morse code tapping of her heart became more urgent. More panicked.

Relax. He won't even be here.

Why would the great Louis come to meet her in person when he had people to send for that?

So was it any wonder that her stomach flipped and twisted when she descended the steps to see him waiting on the runway for her? Perched as he was on the bonnet of a sleek, black car, his impossibly long, muscular legs stretched out in front of him, a crisp suit shirt, sleeves rolled up and open at the neck.

'What are you doing here?'

He grinned, and her stomach knotted some more.

'I trust you had a pleasant flight? Didn't find my private plane too much of an ordeal after all?'

'It was wonderful,' she conceded.

'Bon.'

Before she had time to think, he thrust to his feet, pulling her into his arms and snagging her mouth with his.

It was happening too fast. She wasn't ready.

Her body was on fire with fresh need.

Startled, she pulled away, but his iron grip on her only tightened, his head bending so that only she could hear the mild reprimand. It should have felt threatening, instead it felt thrilling.

'I might remind you that the aim is to show the world that we have fallen madly, desperately in love. We've caught the public interest and we are being observed. All the time.'

'There's no one around,' she choked out, trying to look around.

Louis caught her hair, anchoring her head in place but looking for all the world like a passionate lover.

'Do not look, there is always someone around. The trick is to pretend you don't know they're there.'

'I *don't* know they're there,' she reasoned, wishing her heart would drop back into her chest instead of lodging itself somewhere around her throat.

'There's at least one guy with a long-lens camera on the outer perimeter, on the other side of the runway. The giveaway is the odd glint of sunlight reflected by the glass,' he informed her. 'So kiss me, please. As if you really mean it.'

It may as well have been the excuse her body had been looking for to override any last shred of common sense. Leaning slowly backwards, her eyes meeting Louis's and never leaving them, she dropped her shoulder bag with exaggerated care and then looped her hands around his neck.

'As if I really mean it, you say?' she challenged, proud of the way her voice didn't shake, even once.

His gaze darkened.

'For the camera.'

'Oh, of course.' She quirked her lips, delighting in the flare of desire in his face.

Either he wanted her just like he had the other night, or he was a really, really good actor.

And then she kissed him. Met him. Matched him. Their mouths moved against each other, their tongues dancing a slow, sensual rhumba. This time it was she who eventually broke the contact, seeking out that impossibly square jaw-line until she reached his ear, grazing the lobe with semi-gentle teeth as she moved to the sensitive spot behind it.

His reaction was instant. And evident. Heat pooled between her legs at the unmistakeable feel of him. What *she* had managed to elicit. As though she had some kind of power over him. It was a heady sensation. She lost track of where they were, what was around them and she rocked against him, her body splayed against his.

'*Dieu*,' he growled in her ear, barely catching her hand from sliding down his chest to his trousers. 'Is this where you choose to come to me? Out here, on the tarmac?'

She blinked, crashing back to earth. Remembering where they were.

'I… The photographer,' she whispered hoarsely.

'Has more than enough, believe me.' His voice was harsh, tight. 'Now, get into the car.'

It took everything she had to stay calm and not scramble to get inside, wondering if she'd ever felt so mortified. When Louis joined her on the butter-soft leather she couldn't help her yelp of discomfort. Though she noticed he did nothing to close the gap between them.

'Quite a show,' he accused her.

She had no idea how she managed to raise one eyebrow at him, her voice shockingly level.

'I thought that was the whole point.'

'I asked for a kiss, not an open invitation to take you right there on the runway. *That* part of it is something I'd rather do with you in private.'

'Really? This, from the king of sex spectacles?'

'With other women, Alex,' he bellowed. 'Not with you.'

It sliced her deeper than she'd thought possible. An unambiguous slap in the face of just how gauche, how sexually unsophisticated she was.

So much for keeping her head around him. One minute in his company and she was losing her mind and her morals. It was more confusing than ever. Like being a human pendulum, swinging wildly from one extreme to the other.

Now, like a wounded animal, she retreated to her corner of the car to lick her wounds. Louis, on the other hand, stewed silently in his.

CHAPTER TEN

IT WAS LIKE some kind of illogical torture. Sitting here, at the restaurant, both equally frustrated yet having to flirt, to play the loving couple, just to conceal their row from the other curious diners so that they could forge ahead with the main goal of tonight. To stage their very public engagement.

The timing couldn't have been worse. After this afternoon he was still smarting. *Smarting.* As though their contretemps had actually got to him.

And yet it had. Even now, when he thought back over what had happened on the runway, he couldn't work out where it had all sprung from.

A row.

As if they were a proper couple.

It was almost enough to make him laugh. And somehow the thought chipped the first sharp corner off the block of granite that seemed to have taken up residency in his chest.

'I apologise,' he murmured. 'For what I said to you this afternoon.'

She looked up at him in surprise, then belatedly smiled. To him, it was too brittle to be a real smile, but he knew that, even to fool the hawk-eyed photographers, it would appear to be the sweetest, shyest smile.

'You mean for reminding me how I don't match up to any of the other women you've...*dated?*'

The smile didn't even waver. If anything, he felt it become that much sharper, like a scalpel blade pressed against his chest. But it was her words that had him taken aback. He fought to keep a frown from his face.

'That certainly isn't what I said.'

'Yes, it is.' She nodded vigorously before remembering herself. She leaned forward across the table so no one could possibly overhear them, although they both knew it would simply look as though she was captivated by him.

Incredible how much he suddenly wished that was true.

'You'll have to refresh my memory.'

Her pretty blush would certainly make it into tonight's papers. As would the way she steeled herself, like a woman boosted by love. Like a woman *in* love.

He should be pleased she could play the part so well.

'Fine. You told me you were more than happy to have sex with other women. Just not me.'

He laughed then. To his ears the sound was hollow and full of disbelief, yet the restaurant diners seemed oblivious to the undercurrent at his table. The not-so-covert stares only became all the more indulgent. As if they truly believed they were watching a couple happy to be together.

But what are *they watching?*

He hastily muffled the voice in his head. But it was too late.

'Is that why you were angry? Upset?' He caught her chin in his hands, not too roughly but enough to force her to look at him, to read the truth in his gaze. 'I said I didn't care if the world saw me with any of those other women, or read those ridiculous kiss and tells. But I never wanted the media to gossip about you in that way. You deserve better. However, I did *not* say I didn't want to have sex with you. We both know nothing could be further from the truth.'

She didn't want to believe him so easily. He could read her like the latest medical journal. But she was wavering, and that could only be a good sign. Abruptly, he was filled with the urge to convince her, to reassure her. As though what was between them was real and not just a charade.

'I want you, Alex. Fervently. I want you any way you can imagine, and probably a fair few you can't. You have no idea how close I was to losing myself right out there on that runway. I don't lose myself, Alex. I never lose myself. *That's* why I was so mad.'

'I lost myself, too,' she whispered after a moment, a hot flush blooming on her cheeks.

It was adorable. *She* was adorable.

Before he could stop himself, he leaned across the table and kissed her. Her response was as perfect as it was instantaneous. She made him feel like a king.

'I promised myself I wouldn't go there again.' She smiled ruefully, her eyes sliding to the flashbulbs that were going crazy outside the windows. 'Especially in front of them out there.

It was a jolt to realise that he'd almost forgotten about the press, too caught up in Alex herself. He should take a step, regroup. Only he couldn't, he was enjoying this far too much. He couldn't help it. He toyed with the stem of his glass.

'So what happened?'

'You happened.' She managed to make it sound exciting and irritating at the same time. 'I was all set, I had my speech all prepared…'

He frowned. 'Your speech?'

'About how that morning could only be a one-night stand.'

This time his laugh was genuine, if a little regretful.

'I'd hardly call it that. We got interrupted.'

'Which was a good thing,' she assured him, but the way she refused to meet his eyes told him she didn't even believe her own words.

'Liar.' He slid his hand across the table and took hers. It could have been part of the act, but it wasn't. You wanted that morning as much as I did.'

Her teeth worried at her lip before she offered a sheepish smile.

'Perhaps.'

Sweet. Perfect. Alex.

Before he knew what he was doing, Louis slid out of his seat, his hand drawing the ring box from his inside suit pocket. As though his body knew what he was doing even before his brain did. As though he was acting on instinct and desire, rather than their carefully laid plans.

As though he was only partly playing the part.

And he knew Alex felt it too. The expression on her face certainly wasn't as composed or cool as it would have been if she hadn't been as caught up as he was.

He told himself that it was a good thing that it made their charade all the more convincing.

But that wasn't even the half of it.

'Alexandra Vardy...' The words certainly weren't any he had composed in his head beforehand. They would be relayed from the diners, to the press and around the world within minutes. He told himself that was the point of saying them, but he knew that wasn't entirely true.

'You make me want to be a better man. A better human being.' His voice dipped then, huskier than he might have intended. 'Marry me.'

Her fingers had shot to her mouth, her wide-eyed expression relaxing into one of tentative hope. An unexpected fierceness shot through him; the sense that such open innocence should be cherished. Protected. She gave a halting nod and then she dropped her hands to cup his face. Something shot through him that he couldn't put a name to.

Didn't want to.

And still he couldn't break the moment.

'Say the words, Alex.'

She knitted her eyebrows at him, but he found he couldn't let her off with it; couldn't explain why he needed to hear her say the words.

'Say it,' he murmured.

She opened her mouth, closed it again, and then took a deep breath.

'Yes. Yes, Louis, I'll marry you.'

The fire that burst within him made no sense. Still, he stood up, gathering her into his arms and kissing her as though they were the only two people in the room. In the universe.

A blazing, hot, white light in the middle of darkness.

He might have known it couldn't last.

They were still caught up in his thoughts when the maître d' hurried over, his usual elegant, practised glide all but abandoned, not even attempting to speak in English for Alex, even though he'd been doing so all night.

'I apologise for the interruption but there is an urgent call for you, Monsieur Delaroche. A serious Motocross accident involving young Florien. They think he might die.'

Everything receded from Louis's head. Florien,

the grandson of Arnaud. This was what he, Louis, excelled at—surgery, helping people medically. If there was an accident, Louis intended to be there.

Alex watched Louis, wondering what was going on. His grim expression was one she didn't recognise and his gabbled French was too fast for her to even attempt to understand.

She knew there had been an accident…someone's leg…a fracture maybe. Or a break.

The call he made was brief, factual. Louis was already standing and pulling a wad of notes out of his wallet, his apology curt.

'There's been an accident?' she prompted as he snatched up his jacket.

'I'm sorry, yes. A Motocross accident,' For the first time Louis looked at her. 'Florien, Arnaud's grandson.'

'A crash?'

'He was making a jump when he realised he wasn't going to make it and so he threw himself off the bike. But he didn't throw himself far enough.'

That suggested impact. And if it was the top of his leg, Alex knew it didn't sound good.

'Femur fracture?'

'Could be.' Louis shrugged as they exchanged a grim look. 'It's too dark for them to see if there's any shortening of the leg but I know Florien, he's quite a tough kid. Still, it sounds like he's in incredible pain.'

They both knew that with a femoral break the surrounding muscles would spasm, pulling one end of the broken bone past the other. It *would* be painful but more significantly it could cause bleeding as well as muscle and nerve damage.

The stress of the afternoon, and the euphoria of the proposal, fell away in an instant. Because of the femur's proximity to the femoral artery, it was possible that a patient could haemorrhage to death from an isolated femur fracture. Until they got to Florien they wouldn't have any idea how serious it was.

And Alex had a feeling Louis was about to tell her to stay at the restaurant while the maître d' had someone send a car from the chateau to collect her.

'Forget it,' she told Louis, standing up before he could open his mouth. 'I'm going with you. If it's as serious at you fear then I might be able to help.'

It was almost gratifying that he didn't argue. He simply squeezed her hand, had a quick word with the sombrely nodding maître d' and headed out the door.

She rushed to keep up with him, both of them silent as they jumped into the car. Louis revved the engine into life and they roared away, eventually turning off the road and onto a dirt track barely fit for a dirt bike, let alone a car.

'Hold on,' he advised.

Alex braced herself as the car hurtled over bumps and divots, the bottom of the car grinding worryingly as it hit the ground. Even with Louis's skilled driving it was going to be wrecked. But, then, anyone with less skill than Louis could never have got it over this terrain in the first instance.

She saw kids desperately waving their arms fractions after Louis did. The car pulled up sharply by the boy, barely at a standstill before Louis was out and racing across, the cries of pain letting them know how close Florien was.

The terrain was, frankly, not designed for high-heeled shoes.

Alex gathered up her dress and made her ungainly way behind Louis, who turned abruptly.

'I keep a gym bag in the boot with a change of clothes,' he called out, and then he was gone.

Alex gratefully made her way to the back of the

car, throwing it open and grabbing the bag. A pair of shorts, a T-shirt and a tracksuit greeted her, as well as a welcome pair of socks. Within minutes she was changed and hurrying the short distance across the ground. Even so, she was still a fair way behind Louis and by the time she reached them he was on his phone and barking out instructions in French.

Beyond him, lamps had been placed in a circle, shining light on a young boy lying flat on the ground. But even from that distance there was no doubt it was a femoral break, with one leg significantly shorter than the other and clearly at an unnatural angle. She made her way down the dirt mound.

'Mid-shaft, closed fracture,' Louis informed her as soon as he'd finished on the phone. 'I've updated the emergency services and made sure an air ambulance is on its way. But they're going to need to package him up before they transport him.'

She nodded. 'Straighten the leg and slip the femur back in place, or at least as close as,' she said, her voice quiet.

'We can speed that up for them so they can get him to hospital quicker.'

'You have a traction splint back at the chateau?' she guessed.

'No, we'll make one in the field.'

Her stomach dipped with uncertainty.

'I don't know how.'

'I'll teach you,' he said simply, matter-of-fact.

Despite her reservations, she instantly felt more confident.

'What about pain relief? We can't try to move the leg without anything.'

'In this instance there's no compromise,' he stated. 'I need you to find the materials.'

Quashing any reservations, she nodded her head.

'Okay.'

'Good.' His brief smile filled her with warmth. 'First I need a couple of branches. One should be about a metre and half long to run from his armpit to his foot, the other should be about just under a metre to run from his groin to his foot. Forked, if at all possible.'

'What diameter do you want them, or does it matter?' she hedged.

'They're going to support the leg so I'd say make sure they're sturdy and thick. At least four centimetres.'

'Okay.' She was beginning to get the idea, and Louis's characteristic strength was infectious.

Whatever had happened in town this afternoon, maybe they could put it aside after all.

'You're also going to need to find a stick to go on the underside of his foot and several lengths of something to lash them together. Rip up material if you have to.'

'What about belts? I bet his friends would give us theirs.'

'Good,' Louis said approvingly. 'If we pad the area, that could work. We need to pad the area where the sticks will go so get as much clothing together as you can.'

Galvanised, Alex cast around and grabbed a few of Florien's friends. Telling one of them to start collecting spare coats, jumpers, any clothing he could, and thrusting a lamp into the hands of another so that they'd be able to see what they were looking for, Alex managed to get the others to follow her as she headed to the wooded area a short way away. Once she got there, she could use the branches around her to get across to them what they were looking for. As far as she was concerned, the more eyes there were, the better.

It was easier than she'd expected to find a selection of branches, especially with the help of Florien's desperate friends. Discarding those she knew wouldn't be suitable, they gathered the rest up and headed back to where Louis was to select whichever he thought would work best.

She'd planned to sort out the rest of the clothing once she got there, but was hardly surprised to see Louis already had it in hand, as well as consistently checking on his patient and looking for a pulse. He looked up as soon as she approached.

'Everything okay?'

'Not bad.' She tried not to let her heart kick. 'What about Florien?'

He kept his expression deliberately neutral for those around them, but the look he exchanged with her was one of mutual understanding.

And something else. The former bonds of connection were returning.

'I'll be happier when I get the traction done and there's a good pedal pulse.'

'The branches are there.' She indicated them, understanding his concern. 'Hopefully there'll be some useful lengths in there.'

'Great.'

Reaching over, he ran an expert eye over the selection and then chose two longer pieces, offering each up to the outer side of Florien. Quickly he discarded one and then, after a quick word to the group, which promptly produced an army-style knife, he began to dig out a notch in one end of the other branch.

Alex watched fascinated as he did the same with a shorter branch, offering them up to the boy on either side of the leg requiring traction. Then he began to secure the longer branch to Florien by sliding padding and a belt around the boy's waist.

'Can you reach?'

Hastily, Alex slipped her hand under to find the other end of the belt that Louis was passing under their patient's back, and as she caught on to what he was doing, he left her to it as he moved on to tie another, securing it around the top of the boy's leg, this time including the shorter branch. When she was done at Florian's waist, Alex moved lower, making sure not to tie anything on his knee but keeping well above and below, still padding as she went.

It felt easy and natural to be working together, Alex realised. They instinctively knew each other, could anticipate the other, taking it in turns to soothe Florien and try to reassure him, despite the pain he had to be in. A little of the earlier trust was back. Working together just as they had in Theatre was reminding them both of the connection they'd shared.

At least, Alex hoped it was.

And then they were at the ankle, and Louis produced a long length of bandage.

'First-aid kit in the car.' He half smiled as she glanced at it in surprise. 'I need it for this bit more than anywhere else.'

'You're going to tie the ankle,' she guessed.

'Yes, but watch.'

Curious, Alex observed as Louis tied it around Florien's ankle, then twisted each end around the final small branch, which he fitted under the boy's foot. Then he slid in a winching stick.

'Now.' He leaned in to Alex's ear. 'You twist, I'll deal with Florien. Whatever you hear, keep twisting until his legs are the same length and you know the bone is realigned. The quicker you can do it, the sooner the worst of the pain is over for him, understand?'

Louis was trusting her, depending on her, and that felt good. Not to mention the fact that she wanted to help this poor kid as much as she could. Lifting her eyes briefly to Louis's, she gave a sharp dip of her head.

'Ready,' she murmured.

And then she twisted. Over and over and over, blocking out the sounds of Florien's screams as Louis talked to him and reassured him. She only knew that the smoother and faster she could perform her role, the better in the long run. And then she had done it. His leg was straighter, the femur realigned as close as they were going to get it, given the crude equipment they had, and Florien's legs were the same length.

'Okay.' She raised her voice loud enough for Louis to hear, shaking away the stray hairs that clung to the sweat on her face.

'Nice. Now secure the winching stick so it doesn't reverse and loosen what you've just done, then slip each end of the cross-branch into the notches I made in each of the splint branches.'

'Like this?'

'Exactly,' Louis confirmed, turning back to Florien to confirm to him that it was over. Then he checked the pulse in the boy's toes and foot.

'Good pedal pulse, no swelling, toes are nice and pink. Good result, Alex, well done.'

His praise felt inordinately good, but more than that they'd been working well together and somehow that had eased her discomfort since her arrival better than any gourmet meal could have done.

'Take my car back to the chateau and speak to Brigitte. Florien's mother has already been contacted and is on the way to the hospital but Brigitte will know the best people to call to look after the younger siblings over the next day or so.'

'Okay.'

'And, Alex,' he called softly. 'I'll see you back at home.'

CHAPTER ELEVEN

IT WAS LATER than she'd thought it would be by the time Alex trudged up the stone steps and through the silent chateau. She didn't need to search for Brigitte as the older woman came hurrying from the kitchens as soon as Alex entered. Hugging her and nodding, taking a moment to talk about other things, which left Alex's head spinning, the older woman bustled away. Her parting words were to tell a dazed Alex that a fire had been lit and food set out if she was hungry.

It was a welcome suggestion, especially when the first waves from the blazing fire began to thaw Alex's frozen toes. The engagement ring glinted in the firelight, and a different kind of warmth blew gently through her chest. Despite the long night and the exhaustion beginning to set in, the thought of going to her room without Louis was one she didn't care to entertain.

Louis. The man who would soon be her husband. Her stomach flip-flopped. Their charade aside, if she wasn't marrying playboy Louis, but instead marrying the version of the man she'd seen out there tonight, the man who hadn't thought twice about helping the son of one of his employees, treating him with no less care or respect than he would his top bill-paying patients, then she could actually be the luckiest unconventional bride around.

She quashed the nerves that betrayed her. The fluttering sensation that maybe, just maybe their marriage could be so much more than just a charade. If only she could convince him to stop punishing himself for something he couldn't possibly have had any control over.

Alex froze.

Wasn't that exactly the mistake she'd spent her own life making? *No, it couldn't possibly be the same thing? Could it?* Lost in thought, she collapsed back into the wing-backed chair and stared into the fire.

She didn't know how long she waited, or that she'd even dozed off, but when she awoke Louis was in the room, throwing a couple of logs on the dying fire, the first rays of morning light peeking from around a kink in the heavy curtains.

'What time is it?' She stretched, her neck moving awkwardly.

'Around dawn. You should have gone to bed.'

'I was waiting for you.'

'I accompanied Florien to the hospital.'

Why didn't that surprise her?

'How is he?'

'He'll recover.' Louis nodded grimly.

'But no more Motocross.' She hazarded a smile, unprepared for the shockwaves that coursed through her body as Louis smiled wryly in return.

'Not for a good while. But, knowing Florien, he won't be able to give it up for good.'

'Obstinate, then, just like all young men?'

'We Lefebvre men are the same.'

The room fell silent, only the logs spitting in the fireplace disturbing the air. And Louis's gaze was on her, reaching out to her, although she didn't think he even realised it. The fact that he had just identified himself as Lefebvre rather than Delaroche offered her a glimmer of hope that he was finally beginning to accept he wasn't like his cruel father after all; that he had more of his mother's kindness about him than he realised.

Something skittered through Alex and she unconsciously fingered the ring on her finger. Once

Louis accepted that he didn't need to punish himself any more, he would truly be unstoppable. He could change anything he wanted to—*if* he wanted to—and maybe they could really begin to trust each other.

'You know that's who you are,' she began tentatively.

'Alex…'

She couldn't let him interrupt her. Couldn't let him run away this time—although he would never, in a hundred centuries, believe that was what he was doing.

'You don't have to be either your mother or your father. You can be yourself, and who you are is pretty special, Louis. Or at least could be. You're the best parts of the Lefebvre and Delaroche lineages. You could take up your mother's legacy and create something even more prestigious than the Delaroche Foundation. But, unlike your father, you'd be doing it for all the right reasons.'

His lips pulled into a cold, hard line. But he was still standing there, still listening to her. That had to stand for something.

'This again? Why do you keep pushing this? Just because I helped Florien tonight doesn't make me who you want me to be.'

He was right, she couldn't seem to let it go. But suddenly it felt vitally important. She could tell herself it was her last chance to secure Rainbow House, to make her father realise just how much she would sacrifice to make up for what they had lost, but she suspected it had become more than just that.

She suspected it had become more about Louis, and the way he resisted the good part of himself because he didn't feel he deserved it. He was punishing himself for his mother's death and, for some reason, that hurt *her.* As though layers were being peeled away, from the inside out.

Very much as though *Louis* mattered to her. More than she had ever thought possible.

But that couldn't be right.

This was about her father, and Rainbow House. Nothing more, nothing less, and that was what she had to stick to.

'It isn't who *I* want you to be,' she pressed. 'It's simply who you *are*. You must see that. You're a good man. Everyone who works with you knows that. Brigitte was telling me that only tonight. Every single one of your surgical team, eager to please you every chance they get, knows it. Even the press know you're a good surgeon. They laud you every time you operate.'

'Brigitte said it?'

'Brigitte told me she'd worried when you'd first told them you were bringing someone to the chateau, but that since she's seen us together she hopes our marriage will be a very happy one.'

'Our marriage is a sham.' Louis frowned.

It hurt far more than it should. Alex struggled to answer him.

'Of course I know that. But the point remains, people want the best for you. Did you know she also told me that she knew we were trying to regain control of the Lefebvre Group?'

'There's no such thing as secrets in a place like this.' Louis shrugged, his shuttered expression only heightening her frustration.

'According to Brigitte, your mother once intended for the stable blocks here at the chateau to be turned into a respite centre. Holidays for families from places like Rainbow House and the other charities sponsored by the Lefebvre Group.'

'Is that so?'

Louis gritted his teeth. It was a warning she should heed, but she couldn't. Or she didn't want to.

'It is. Brigitte said your mother even got planning permission, and that your father signed documents to that effect.'

'My father would have long since got rid of any such papers.'

'Not if your mother lodged them at her own solicitors. In trust.'

It was a dangerous game, but she couldn't seem to stop. Aside from their silly argument, things had seemed so positive between them before they'd got the message about Florien. And even then, they'd worked together harmoniously, just as they always did. She felt as close to Louis as she was likely to get.

So why did that knowledge deflate her so?

'Let me guess, Brigitte thinks that, too.'

'Right.' Alex nodded, shoving her misgivings aside. 'You could reinstate your mother's plans and make it one of the first successes of the Lefebvre Group.'

'And call it Rainbow House the Second? Maybe Rainbow Court?' His anger was apparent. 'Alex, how many times can I tell you that I don't want to take over the Lefebvre Group? Or the Delaroche Foundation. The Lefebvre Group was my mother's drive, her passion, because it was something away from my father. But to me, it holds too many bad memories. The Delaroche Foundation has only ever been a vehicle for my father to gain a knighthood. It has never been about helping people, for him.'

'So you can be different.' She stood up, took a step forward and then stopped, her arms dropping to her sides helplessly as Louis folded his own arms across his chest as though warding her off.

'No. I am who I am. I'm a brilliant surgeon…' he shrugged as though it was a fact he acknowledged but wasn't boasting about '…but I'm not a good man. I tried to make sure I was nothing like my father, yet everything I've done has made me more like him with every day.'

'You mean the playboy nonsense,' she sniffed. 'Why do you insist on punishing yourself with that? It's only a part of who you were, not even who you are now. You're a surgeon above all else. You have determination, persistence, passion.'

'For surgeries, Alex. I have that passion for surgeries. I could carry out procedures day and night and I would never tire of them because they inspire me and every surgery is different. But the Lefebvre Group was my mother's passion and her footsteps don't lead somewhere I want to follow.

I don't even like the man I become when I think of that place and everything it took from us.'

'So if you don't like that man you become, change him. Turn it into something positive. If anyone can achieve that, it's you, Louis.'

'It wouldn't be enough,' he said abruptly. 'Do you think this is the first time I've regretted some of my choices? Those first kiss-and-tell encounters that gave me the reputation as a playboy? I'd been trying to hurt my father, damage the Delaroche name, make people look twice and realise that Jean-Baptiste wasn't their knight-in-shining-scrubs, but a brilliant surgeon with a grubby personal life of his own.'

'You were eighteen. We all make stupid choices when we're younger—sometimes when we're older too—but most of us don't do it in the public eye where it follows us around for years to come.'

'That's hardly the point,' he ground out angrily, but it was the pain behind it that clawed at Alex, deep inside. 'I'm not *most* people. I'm Louis Delaroche. My grandfather was a Lefebvre. I should have known better.'

'You lost your mother,' she exclaimed, 'your guide, over ten years earlier! By your own admission your father was hardly the greatest role model.'

'I don't want to enough.' He shook his head. 'I'm selfish, just like him. I know the Lefebvre Group needs a chairman, and I know that was meant to be my role. It was what my mother always wanted me to do. But I don't want any part of it because I can't get past my own hurt. I'm angry with my father for his affairs, which drove my mother to the edge, and I'm angry with her for choosing the way out that she did. Most of all, I'm angry with myself that I wasn't good enough to give her something to hold onto.'

It was the most honest he'd been with her and something sang inside her at the knowledge. She was desperate to go to him, to hold him, but she didn't dare move for fear of breaking the moment. A minute ago they'd been standing across the room from each other, only a few metres but it might as well have been a yawning chasm, and now suddenly it felt like he'd thrown the first rope across the divide. The first step to building a bridge.

The logs spattered and a clock chimed in the entrance hall, the sound echoing along the silent chateau corridors.

It was only when Louis exhaled, moving as though he was about to turn and leave, that Alex finally spoke.

'I do understand your guilt, Louis. You blame yourself for your mother's death. I know what it's like to carry around a burden of responsibility that isn't your own.'

'Your brother.' He blinked, as though remembering it for the first time.

She swallowed, her heart accelerating uncontrollably.

'Not just my brother. My mother, too.'

Louis stilled, his jaw locked, the pulse ticking away the only tell-tale sign that he wasn't as calm as he would have her believe.

'You don't. Not like this. I know you mean well, but these are my demons.'

Shutting her out like he always shut out everyone. Leaving her no choice but to go to the one place she'd swore she would never go. Even now, she knew it would cost her.

She hoped Louis was worth the risk.

'I never told you how my mother died, did I?' she heard herself say.

And suddenly there it was, the pain that was always there—like a dull ache that never, ever went away—but now it was rearing up, sharper and more biting than it had felt in years.

She stuffed it back down and forced herself to meet Louis's gaze, her momentary pause losing her what little advantage she might have had. He raked a hand through his hair.

'Alex, I don't want to get into a "my pain is worse than your pain" contest. I'm just explaining to you why I don't want to take on the Lefebvre Group.'

'And I'm just telling you how my mother died,' she managed quietly, her fingers gripping her book so he couldn't see how she was shaking.

The air thrummed with tension, breath bated to see who would fold first.

Eventually, Louis dipped his head in perceived acquiescence, moving around the chair and flopping down to lounge in his deliberately insouciant fashion.

She drew in a slow, discreet breath and counted to ten before uttering the words she hadn't said for decades.

'My mother died in childbirth. After she'd been in labour with me. The child who had been conceived as a potential saviour sibling for their son, but who would turn out not to be a match, was also the direct cause of her mother's death. So, you see, I do understand a thing or two about guilt and responsibility.'

She hated that look he shot her then. The look of pity. The one she'd grown to resent so much as a kid that she'd started telling people her mother had died in a car accident.

'Don't look at me like that, Louis.'

She braced herself for the platitudes.

'How? How did she die?'

As though he could read her. She cast him a ghost of a grateful smile.

'Placenta percreta. The placenta had grown through the uterine wall and invaded her bladder. They couldn't do anything. Everything ruptured and she bled out.'

'I'm sorry. I can't imagine...'

'I content myself with the knowledge that she got to hold me, at least for a few moments. And she told my father to love me and made him promise to tell me every time I needed him to that she was grateful for the chance to meet me.'

'Did he?'

'No. He never told me. He tried to, in his own way, but he couldn't bear talking about her. In the end it was my grandparents who used to tell me but it wasn't the same. I always felt he blamed me, deep down. And so I blamed myself. When my brother died, my father retreated even more and so I took on that responsibility, too.'

He shook his head, his fist balled as though he was angry on her behalf. As if he wanted to protect her.

As if he *cared.*

'I didn't tell you this because I wanted your sympathy.' She made her voice crisp, unemotional, telling herself that she'd dealt with that pain even though she could still feel it, rattling the heavy chains on its prison door, even now.

'I told you because I wanted to show you that I let that experience drive me to become a doctor. To become someone she would have been proud of. I know you play the bad boy because you think it's somehow your punishment, but honestly I think that's nonsense.'

She knew he was about to stop her but she held her hand up to silence him. If she didn't tell him now, she'd never get the chance to say it.

'You were seven, a child. You can't hold yourself responsible for someone else's happiness. You could be doing so much more. Even if you can't do it for her, you owe it to yourself to be the kind of man you have the potential to be. If only you'd forgive yourself.'

He'd only felt helpless once before in his life. The night his mother had turned her back on him.

Louis was determined tonight wasn't going to be the second time.

But seeing Alex so distressed, and knowing how worthless her father had made her feel—not by hurling the kind of vicious jibes that his own father had but by staying silent and withholding his love—made Louis furious, powerless and mournful all at once.

And yet he couldn't let her off so easily.

'You talk about me forgiving myself. But have you?'

He could tell by the rush of panic in her eyes that he was right.

'Of course. That's why I can volunteer at Rainbow House. I've confronted my ghosts.'

'I don't buy that, Alex. I know you volunteer to maintain that last connection with your father. But if you forgave yourself then you wouldn't need to hang onto him. You'd tell yourself that it was time he met you halfway.'

'Who said I didn't enjoy volunteering there for myself?' she blustered.

'You. You've never once given that as a reason. You've always linked it to your father.'

She stilled. He thought she'd even stopped breathing. Then she blinked rapidly, as if tears were stinging her soulful eyes, and guilt poured through him.

'I'm sorry, I shouldn't have said that.'

'But you were right,' she whispered. 'I'm just as tethered to my past as you are. I wanted to help you see that you weren't helping anyone by punishing yourself. I thought I could help you move on.'

He didn't remember standing up or crossing the room to scoop her into his arms. But suddenly they were there together and all he could do was to hold her body close to his, try to make her feel safe and secure. And cared for.

So what did that mean?

He let the question wash over him as her blinks gave way to the first silent tears. He carried her out of the door, up the grand, sweeping staircase and to her room. And he let her hold onto him as if she would never let go as he settled her on the bed, nodded wordlessly when she begged him not to leave her, lay down beside her and cradled her as sobs racked her, crying for probably the first time in decades. Finally allowing herself to grieve for the things she'd lost as well as the things she'd never had. Finally letting go after years of trying to build bridges with her father and holding her feelings inside.

And when the tears at last began to ebb and the hiccups subside, when, exhausted and depleted, her eyes tired and swollen, sleep crept over her, he continued to hold her. Long after the house fell silent and the fire died in the hearth. Long into the night until the tendrils of slumber wisped around him. Right into the first hints of light and the sounds of the dawn chorus.

As his eyes began to open again, Louis tipped his head from one side to the other to ease the crick in his neck. After last night he ought to feel drained. Wary, even. Instead, he just felt as though a weight had finally been lifted from him. Hearing Alex share her story with him and knowing she hadn't told anyone else had changed things for him somehow.

Suddenly, he no longer felt the isolation he'd never realised he'd been experiencing. His brain was fired up with renewed drive. An energy effervescing in blood that coursed eagerly through his veins. If he could only work out what to do with it.

He'd spent years playing genius, playboy Louis, convinced there was a reason that he was renowned for his surgical skills on the one hand and his sexual prowess on the other. But the truth was that he'd been little different from any other nineteen-year-old kid with money and women throwing themselves at him. The only thing that set him apart was the name he'd been forging for himself in the surgical field.

The press had only jumped on the playboy story because it had sold more papers for them. And he'd let them because it had seemed easier. Because it had been convenient. But Alex made him want something different. Something...*more.*

Maybe, and he wasn't saying definitely, taking on the role of Chairman of the Lefebvre Group was something he should consider. Maybe he and Alex could make their sham marriage work for them, and pull together to really achieve something good. Maybe their marriage could be more than just... *No, that was going too far.*

But still they could make a good business team. No one else could ever have dared to talk to her the way he had last night. He, in turn, could never have trusted anyone else with the truths he'd told her this past week.

Easing his hand from under her neck, Louis slid off the bed, covering her with a blanket and taking his time so as not to disturb her. The hot, powerful jets of the shower sluiced over his body and, with it, any residual anhedonia of the previous night, of the previous decade.

He barely brushed the towel over his body before pulling on jeans and a tee, clothes that he hadn't worn in years but which welcomed him from the back of his burr-walnut wardrobe. Louis snatched up his phone, his fingers scrolling efficiently through old contact numbers. With a final glance at Alex's sleeping form, he slipped out of the room.

It was well into the morning before Alex appeared, having tracked him down to where he was meeting someone in the east wing drawing room. She looked as deliciously fresh and bewitching as ever. He forced himself not to stare at her.

'I'm sorry.' She backed up immediately. 'I didn't realise you were in a meeting.'

'Don't leave.' He waved his hand immediately

to beckon her over. 'Étienne is just leaving, we were finishing up anyway.'

She only hesitated for a moment before advancing with a sweet smile, her hand outstretched in greeting as the man dropped a light kiss on her hand, making his introductions and apologies as he excused himself to run to another meeting.

'Étienne Morel is a lawyer. His father was my mother's personal lawyer, who never had much time for Jean-Baptiste.'

'You're looking into what Brigitte said last night,' she breathed, the expectation dancing in her eyes almost too much for him to stand.

'I'm making tentative enquiries, shall we say,' he cautioned. 'I cannot promise anything. I will not promise. Don't get ahead of yourself, Alex. I am simply…weighing the options.'

He could see by her body language that his words were falling on deaf ears but her delight got under his skin in a way that wasn't prudent and, if only for a short while, he gave in to the temptation of indulging her.

'Étienne's also looking into finding the Lefevbre Group tie-in with the Delaroche Foundation—maybe fresh eyes can see a loophole. In the meantime, he found the plans Brigitte mentioned easily enough. The idea was to convert the old stables into small holiday apartments for disabled people and carers. They already had made provisions for wheelchair access and additional security features.'

He waited with a strange tenseness as she perused the drawings, her finger tracing every last inch of space, her soft voice reading the French aloud, translating.

'Right. Accessibility but with more practicalities. This could be safety gates, well-fenced gardens, and ensuring doors and windows can be locked to prevent any little Houdinis.'

'Perhaps building a couple of swimming pools but ensuring they were both secured.'

'Perfect.' The look she sent him pulled straight down to his sex. He thrust it away. 'For some families it might be more about assuring them that they're coming somewhere safe and secure, and assuring them they can relax in the knowledge that no one is going to be judging them.'

'I also considered respite holidays,' he said, searching her expression.

'Proper respite holidays?' Alex asked slowly. 'Where the carers also get a proper holiday, not just a bit of break?'

'Why not?' he challenged. 'We could offer twenty-four-hour nursing care, attracting qualified, highly experienced nursing and care staff if we refurbished the west wing of the house and turned it into high-spec accommodation. Furthermore, this estate has always provided plenty of work for the surrounding communities, and the decline since my father took over has hit people around here hard. We could also run annual courses to train suitable locals or anyone else willing to come here.'

'You could offer quality hospitality,' she mused. 'A relaxed atmosphere with plenty of excursions and lively entertainment?'

'Right.'

'Is there a lot to do around here?'

The grin curved his lips and her eyes darkened, intensified as she watched him. It was dangerous ground. He needed to back away.

He couldn't.

'I think you should take a tour of *our* little town and its environs.'

CHAPTER TWELVE

'SO THIS IS the Canal du Midi?'

'This is the Canal du Midi in style,' Louis corrected, pouring her another wine as their sleek boat cruised leisurely along.

This day was driving him slowly mad.

Or, more to the point, Alex was.

Despite all his words of caution to himself, his constant reminders that their engagement was one of convenience and not choice, he found himself sucked into the charade that the press were lapping up everywhere they went. And showing Alex around his town, the place in which he had grown up, and seeing her obvious pleasure at some of the sights that had so captivated him as a child wasn't making the task any easier. Her freely given smiles, the way she charmed everyone he introduced to her, her uninhibited laughter.

He'd watched her. And he'd wanted her.

The small canal boat ride had been her idea. He'd loved it as a kid but his tastes had run to more refined, elegant super-yachts in the last few decades. Sitting here with Alex, he couldn't help but wonder why.

They'd moored to take a stroll to a canal-side patisserie for an impromptu lunch of baguette and some local produce. Right now she was taking long gulps from a bottle of ice-cold water, the long line of her neck making him think of anything other than the history lesson about seventeenth-century canals that he was meant to be giving her.

Worse, Alex was apparently oblivious as she screwed the top back on her water and set it down to look around them.

'Why are there so many felled trees around this area?'

'They're diseased, they needed to be felled,' he said ruefully.

She looked aghast and it felt better than it should. Seeing her care about some of things that he cared about, as though they were in perfect sync.

But they weren't. It was all pretence. So why was that so hard to remember?

'All of them? Why?'

'They were plane trees, planted back in the early nineteenth century to strengthen the banks and to help prevent evaporation, since they grow rapidly and they furnish quick shade.'

'So they've been here around two hundred years? Why on earth would you cut them down now?'

'No choice.' He hunched his shoulders. 'Over the last decade or so it's become clear that many of them were diseased, possibly from a fungus brought to France in contaminated World War II ammunition boxes used by US troops. Plus boat users often lash ropes around the trees to moor their boats and as they moved up and down the canal it no doubt helped the disease to spread.'

'So they're taking out this whole section and replanting.' Alex pulled a face. 'So many trees.'

'More than you think, since it isn't just this section. So far over twenty thousand trees have been felled along the two-hundred-and-fifty-kilometre canal length but there's a real chance that all forty-two thousand of them will ultimately need to go.'

Her cry was typically heart-on-sleeve Alex. And he loved her for her passion.

'That's awful. All of them?'

'If something is diseased and corrupting, then doesn't it make sense to eradicate it completely? Before you can start again?'

He hadn't intended it, yet it seemed to spill off his tongue. She peered at him tentatively.

'Are we still talking about the trees here?'

'What else?' he stalled, trying to gain himself time to think.

She pursed her lips before plunging on.

'I don't know. You?'

She expected him to deny it, to scoff at her. He could see it in her expression. Instead, he met her intelligent gaze head on and they lapsed into silence, the ducks on the canal the only sound.

'So…' She broke the silence at last. 'If they all are felled then they would need to be replaced… but what would be the cost?'

He cocked his head to one side. To anyone listening, it would sound like a dry conversation. Only he could hear the quiver in her voice, and could feel the waves of desire coursing between them. The heat, the solitude, the setting, they were all conspiring to remind them both of the attraction that had been there from the start. The one that they'd spent the last few weeks quashing but which was now, inexplicably, back and seemingly stronger than ever.

'For the trees? Millions. It's a huge undertaking.'

'And for you?'

'I'm still working that out. But I already know the gain is peace of mind. And you.'

He looked so confident, so unruffled. While for her part she seared.

She wanted to move but she couldn't. Part of her expected him to reach for her, but he didn't.

The moment stretched out, circling around them, encompassing only the two of them. When he spoke, his breezy tone scratching over her, it was as though they had never touched on such a topic.

'Still, this isn't what we're here for. I just wanted to show you how we could offer canal cruises, either as a group or partnering some of the small boat-hire companies operating in the area.'

It amazed her the way he could switch so easily but she couldn't shake the moment with the same ease. Louis was a different man. No longer anything like the arrogant playboy of the media and, with each passing day, it was getting harder and harder for Alex to remember that they were still supposed to be playing a game. A charade.

And, if only for one afternoon, she desperately wanted to stop fighting the attraction.

'What if, right in this instant, I'm less interested

in what the region has to offer and more interested in what you have to offer?' she hedged, nervous exhilaration flooding through her.

He eyed her slowly.

'And are you?'

'Am I what?' she mumbled, scorched by the heat of his stare.

His lips quirked upwards.

'Interested in what I have to offer? Because if you are, there's a bed in the cabin in there that I've never used before.'

Was it really that simple?

She just had to ask him? Abruptly her body felt too tight, too constricting for her bones. She wasn't sure how she persuaded her shaking legs to stand, but suddenly she was in Louis's arms.

The best place she'd been in a while.

'No one else has ever got to me the way you do,' he muttered. 'I must be crazy.'

'We both must be,' she breathed, her skin scorching everywhere he touched her, even through their clothing.

'If I'd realised taking you on a guided tour would make you want me, I'd have done it a week ago.'

'It isn't the guided tour,' she squeaked. He knew exactly what he was doing, moving his mouth so close to hers without actually kissing her. Like some exquisite form of torture. 'Talking isn't some kind of foreplay, you know.'

'I know exactly what foreplay is,' he rumbled. 'Allow me to demonstrate.'

And then he kissed her. Or more like possessed her, staking his claim and making her his. And she would be, she realised. In a heartbeat she would be with him. She was *in love* with him. Even if everything with Rainbow House fell through now, she would still marry him. If he asked. Which, of course, he wouldn't.

But she could fantasise. She could press herself against him and loop her arms around his neck, every inch of her body pressed against him.

His for the taking.

Louis claimed her mouth, investing every slide of his lips and every stroke of his tongue with all the promise he intended to fulfil for the rest of the night. The rest of their stay. The rest of the charade.

He thrust any other unwanted thoughts of it ever having to come to an end from his head, cupping her face in his hands, taking his time to explore every single element of it. From the soft, plump lips to the tiny dints in her cheeks that were only visible when she really laughed.

God, he loved to make her laugh so hard that those dimples showed.

Just for him.

He staunched the ferocity that consumed his insides, forcing himself to slow down. Reacquainting himself with her every curve and dip, revelling in the way her body quivered against him when he ran his hand up and down her spine, thrilling in the soft sounds that seemed to vibrate from her throat straight into his chest as he cupped her backside, knowing he was making her melt.

He took his time, plundering her mouth, exploring her face and her neck with his kisses, not even attempting to stifle his grin as she moved against him, her body clearly urging him to do more. His hand tangled into her soft, flowing hair, twisting a lock around his fist and tugging, only gently but enough to make her gasp and press against him harder.

He was too consumed with kissing her. He tested first one breast and then the other, before dropping feather-light kisses from her neck downwards until he was hooking a finger over the neckline of her sexy dress and taking the first straining rosy bud in his mouth. He hardened instantly at her gasps of pleasure. Need almost overtaking him for the first time in his life, he just about remembered they were still on the deck of the boat. Although the footpath was deserted for now, people could walk past at any time.

He'd never lost himself like that before. It felt good. Still, Louis made himself scoop her into his arms, carry her into the cabin to the compact bedroom, and lower her reverently on the bed. Slowly, deliberately, he stripped her, but then she pushed herself up with a litheness he couldn't help but admire and tugged him towards her so that she could hurry things along. Her shaking fingers fumbled with his buttons as she shed him of his clothing, too. And when she unzipped him, her hands moving greedily to his length, Louis lost all attempts at easy control.

'Even more beautiful than I remembered,' he muttered, his hands gliding over her soft skin when they were both finally naked, her body reacting to his touch.

He pressed her back onto the bed, only too happy to follow as her hands snagged his shoulders and she pulled him down to her.

Propping himself on one arm, his eyes skimmed

over her, drinking her in, gorging themselves on her. Everything about Alex was so sweetly feminine, from her crooked, nervous smile—which only served to stoke him further—down to the perfect flare of her hips. His hands traced whorls on her body, his lips moving over hers before dropping hot kisses to her neck, her chest. Her smooth flesh was so delicate to the touch.

Louis revelled in the way her fingers explored his body, moving over his shoulders, his arms and his chest. But what he really remembered, what he ached for was to taste her again as he had that night. Her sweet honey taste that had ensured he had been hooked from the moment he'd first licked his way into her.

He grew harder at the memory. So hard it was almost painful. No one had ever driven him this wild before.

He shifted, preparing to slide back down between her legs when Alex decided she had other plans and shifted herself, trying to roll him over until his chest was over hers. He could have resisted, carried on with his plan. Instead he relented and gave her what she wanted, moving over until his chest covered hers, his body between her impossibly long legs.

And then she wriggled her hips, settling him at her apex and then wrapping her legs around his thighs as though anchoring him in place, and Louis lost the ability to think straight.

He'd intended a slow seduction. Tasting, toying, teasing. Instead desire consumed him, a slave to his most primal instincts, and to Alex's urgency.

The only time any woman had come close to being the master of him.

If he didn't slide inside her now, she was going to die from need.

She was certain of it.

The last few days since their encounter in his bedroom had been unbearable. Every fibre of her body still mourned what hadn't quite happened between them. And now he wanted her, that much was undeniable, yet still he insisted on setting a cruelly controlled pace. The tantalising moves of a rhumba when all her entire body ached for the driven, passionate pace of a tango.

She arched her hips and rocked against him, her already molten body searing as his sex flexed against her, his sharp intake of breath like a roar inside her head. Why was he holding back, tormenting them both this way? Louis was barely in control himself—at least she could take some small comfort from that.

'Please,' she whispered, curving her body into his, the stunning beauty of his physique with the planes and ridges almost too much to process. And when he nudged at her entrance again she was sure she was going to come apart.

His gaze snagged hers and she wasn't prepared for the fire that raged in their smoky depths. Savage, needy and wholly, utterly male.

'I can't take any more.' She bit out the desperate plea.

'I want us to take our time,' he rasped, reaching to retrieve a condom and sheathing himself. But she didn't miss the slight shake to his voice. It gave her strength.

'We've got all night, all week to take our time. I've been imagining you since that morning, I just need you now.'

Her voice cracked before she could say any more but it didn't matter. It was as if she'd uttered the magic words. Told him what he'd been waiting to hear. With a groan Louis shifted, testing himself against her, his face tightening at her slick, wet heat. It filled her with old Alex courage, a kind of mischievousness, an impulse, and she raised her legs to wrap them higher around his body, drawing him in faster than he'd intended.

She didn't know whether the guttural sound came from Louis or from her. In truth, it made little difference. He was thrusting into her, filling her, stretching her in every direction, but there was no discomfort. If anything, it felt as though they were made for each other.

The perfect fit.

He drew back and thrust in again. A deliberate, lazy rhythm that drove her half-mad with pleasure and frustration. Again and again he slid in and out of her, and just when she thought she couldn't take any more teasing, he picked up the pace, leaving her little choice but to grip his shoulders and let him take her with him, meeting him thrust for glorious thrust and trying to remember to breathe.

Shudders were already beginning to burst through her when he slid his hand between their bodies and down to her core, expert fingers dancing over the very centre of her desire, heightening everything and propelling her towards the edge. Then she catapulted off, bursting apart under his skilful touch and crying out his name.

She hadn't even come back down when she realised he hadn't followed her. He was still inside her, still in control of himself, if only by a thread.

'Louis…'

'Shh,' he growled, a dark, deeply satisfied smile lifting his mouth. 'Hold on tightly.'

Before she could answer, he was moving inside her again. Thrusting harder, faster, deeper, his fingers still playing with her, sending her hurtling back over the edge. And this time when her body shattered into a thousand fragments, her muscles rippling around him, he toppled with her.

It took her long, long moments to come back to herself again, and when she did, Louis was cradling her as though she was the most precious jewel in the world.

'You're so beautiful,' he murmured. 'So perfect.'

'So are you.' Still in a haze of bliss, Alex barely heard the words slipping so naturally from her lips. 'I love you.'

Beside her, Louis froze. And then her world came tumbling down.

'You do not love me.' Louis bundled her off him so fast that she almost fell and he nearly put a hand out to catch her, only just stopping himself in time. 'You cannot. That isn't what we agreed.'

If he'd thought she was going to crumble, to fall, then he'd thought wrong. But a part of him had known that she wouldn't. Not his Alex. He admired the way she tilted her chin, meeting his eyes even as she tugged the tangle of sheets over her chest to protect what little modesty she had left. It made his chest tighten with something that felt dangerously close to regret.

'No.' Her soft voice wrapped around him, hot and tight, just as she'd wrapped around his sex only minutes earlier. 'it wasn't what we agreed. And yet here we are.'

'I won't accept that.' He tugged his jeans on furiously.

That, surely, was the point. *Sex.* She was confusing sex with love. And so, to some degree, was he. Why else did he want to pull away all the barriers between them and crush her body until they were so close he didn't know where he ended and she began?

Alex merely shrugged lightly, her hurt evident, and yet she refused to apologise.

'It isn't your choice to make, it's mine. And it appears I've made it. But tell me, Louis, what are you so afraid of?'

He snorted. An ugly sound.

'I'm not afraid of anything. Or anyone.'

'I think you are,' she pressed. 'I think you're afraid of the one person who truly counts. Yourself. You're afraid to be that good surgeon version of yourself because, for some reason, you can't allow yourself to be happy. And so you keep throwing the two-dimensional playboy side out for the world. Why do you do that? Are you afraid you won't measure up to the man you ought to be? And so you won't even try in case you fail?'

It was too close to the mark. He couldn't bear it.

Every time she talked to him like this she made him feel more and more like he could be the man he should have been from the start. She made him *want* to be. If only for her. But now it was too late. He was too like his father. He destroyed things, he didn't create them.

'You think you know me, just because we slept together?' He shook his head. 'How many other women do you think have been exactly where you are now, Alex?'

It was cruel. He had to slide his eyes away so that he didn't see the pain clouding hers. But it was the only way. He couldn't give Alex what she wanted. He wouldn't.

She hoped he would take on the Lefebvre Group,

guide it, nurture it. In her mind, he could build the Lefebvre Group into the force that the Delaroche Foundation could have been if not for his father's ego. How was it she couldn't see that his own ego was just as out of control? That, despite every choice he'd ever made—*because* of every choice he'd ever made—he had turned himself into the one thing he most loathed. He was his father's own son.

She couldn't be allowed to love him. He would end up destroying her. Just as his father had destroyed his mother. It was inevitable.

'This was sex, Alex. Just sex.' The lie practically lodged itself in his throat. 'This is exactly who I am and I *am* happy with that. But since you insist on reading more into it than that, it cannot happen again. We will marry, as agreed, I'll gain control of the Lefebvre Group and I'll appoint a new board to pass it on to, to ensure that Rainbow House, and any other assets, are protected.'

'So you want to protect your mother's legacy from your father, yet not get your hands dirty?' It was the sad, almost sympathetic edge to her tone that really twisted in his chest the most.

He gritted his teeth. Alex must never know how much it cost him to answer her.

He'd been foolish to let himself get caught up in their charade, allowing himself to think, even for a moment, that there was anything real to it. He'd been stupid to allow her to convince him to look into the stable block conversion that his mother had once planned. And he'd been reckless to even consider taking over the role of Chairman of the Lefebvre Group and appointing a board of his own.

He needed to get back to the original plan. Stop his father from destroying his mother's legacy and then walk away. Run, if he had to.

'That's exactly what I intend to do,' he growled, unsure whether he was more furious at her or himself. 'Now get dressed, we're leaving. You have a dress fitting and I have a life to get back to once this is over.'

CHAPTER THIRTEEN

THE NEXT FEW days bled into each other, a tense blur for Alex, until one week stretched into two, then three.

Gone was the Louis who had caused her to abandon herself to the wanton desire that had seemed to fuel them both equally. The Louis who had taught her to revel in his obsession with her body as he'd licked and kissed and tasted his way over every last square centimetre of her trembling flesh.

They had reached an uneasy truce following their argument. They'd had to. Not only for the paparazzi but also for the estate hands and chateau staff, none of whom could be allowed to suspect there was any animosity between the soon-to-be-wed couple.

Alex was almost grateful for the whirlwind of planning and decisions, from her wedding dress to the music, the flowers to the food. At least they kept her mind occupied and the pain at bay.

But it wasn't always so easy. When Louis showed her around the estate, ostensibly so that he could teach his future bride about its history, and how the estate had employed people from the local area for centuries, she could almost fool herself into thinking it was real all over again. Especially when he so proudly recounted to her how his great-grandfather had been unmasked and hunted down as one of the most effective, dogmatic leaders of the Resistance during the Second World War, and local farmers had been prepared—only too willing—to conceal and protect such a man as Albert Delaroche on their farms, even after several of them had been tortured or taken prisoner.

But when she called her father, after she had finally been granted permission to advise him of the highly guarded date of the wedding, she wasn't prepared for what he had to say.

By the time Louis returned, Alex still hadn't moved from the chair by the window, her mobile phone still clasped in her hand. He knew something was wrong the moment he walked in, the immediate concern etched onto his face only making her feel worse.

He strode across the room and for a moment she

thought he was going to haul her out of the chair and into his arms.

Ridiculous notion.

Instead, Louis stopped dead in front of her.

'Did something happen? Did your father upset you?'

She shook her head.

'He didn't like the respite holiday idea? Rainbow Court?'

She'd turned the words over and over in her mind all afternoon, but they still didn't come any easier. There was no soft way to put it. She just had to tell him.

'I told my father we had set a date, I explained. He thanked me for letting him know.'

But he hadn't congratulated her, or celebrated with her, or anything really. He'd just listened politely, thanked her and then, to her surprise, he'd asked her if she was doing it to save Rainbow House. She couldn't tell Louis that she'd harboured some secret fantasy he might tell her that wasn't something she needed to do. At least, not for him. Maybe tell her he did love her, and that she should only marry Louis if she wanted to.

No, she couldn't tell Louis. She could barely

admit that to herself. Alex shook her head as if to dislodge the fanciful idea.

'He did tell me something about your mother.'

'My mother?'

The sense of foreboding swelled up inside her even though she tried to quell it. He waited in silence for her to continue.

'He asked why you had never taken up your role as chairman of the Lefebvre Group before now. I told you Jack was at Rainbow House around the time your mother used to visit regularly?'

'Yes, yes.' He shrugged irritably, but she got the sense there was more going on beneath the surface. If only he would let her in.

But he never would.

'Apparently your mother's desire for you to take over was widely known.'

'Indeed?'

'Well, my father knew her well, Jack was around seven and your mother was very involved with the residents.'

'I am aware of that.'

'Well, we were talking…' If one could call their conversation *talking* in that sense. She flicked a tongue out over parched lips. 'Conversation got around to your mother's death and…basically he said she didn't take her own life. That it was an accident.'

He raked his hand through his hair. In that moment it seemed floppier and more playboyish than ever. It also made him seem more vulnerable than ever and her heart twisted and knotted.

'Yes. Your father would think that. They told everyone it was an accident.'

'No.' She was explaining this badly. 'I mean, I know that. What I mean is, it really *was* an accident.'

He stared at her, first in disbelief, then in exasperation.

'They covered it up, I told you that. It was the only decent thing my father ever did for her.'

'You're wrong. He didn't cover anything up. That is...he did, but not your mother's suicide. It really was an accident. My father was there. He saw exactly what happened.'

Cold fingers inched over her body. She hated the way he looked at her, as though she was lying, deliberately trying to hurt him. How could he think that?

'I saw the photographs, Alex,' he bit out coldly. 'The evidence. Or the lack of it. I know there was a cover-up.'

'There was. But not how you think.'

She touched his arm but he pulled away, unable to bear the contact. Something inside her shrivelled up even smaller. But she couldn't stop now, she had to tell him what she knew.

'Louis, your mother died trying to save someone's life.'

He froze, waiting for her to go on.

'There was a single mother, twenty-three, and her six-year-old daughter. The daughter was severely disabled and the young mother had borderline learning difficulties herself. That particular day it all got too much for her. She went to the child's room and smothered her in her sleep. She was in the process of taking her own life when your mother went past the room and spotted them. Celine hit the alarm and then ran in to try to save the woman by hoisting her up, but her body was convulsing and your mother got knocked over.'

'My mother fell?' It didn't even sound like his voice.

'She hit her head on the metal corner of the bed as she went down. By the time the ambulance crew got to her, she was already gone.'

'It was an accident?'

'Yes. My father was there. He'd heard her in

the refectory barely a few hours before, talking about you as usual, he said.' She reached a tentative hand out to hold his arm again.

This time he didn't move away or throw her off, he simply stared at it. Seeing but not seeing. She doubted he could feel anything at all. She could only imagine he felt numb.

'She always talked about you, apparently,' Alex continued softly. 'She told people you were her whole world. Her *petit prince.*'

He actually staggered back. *Him*, Louis Delaroche. And in that moment Alex knew if she could have taken his pain on in his stead, she would have.

She loved him. And that would cause her far more pain than her father had ever caused her.

Anguish ripped through Louis, like something yanking him in a million different directions at once. He'd forgotten that, her affectionate nickname for him. She'd called him her prince and he'd told her she was more beautiful than even the Princess of England who she had always so loved.

How could he have forgotten?

'They covered it up,' he managed at last, his voice sounding so, so far away. Lost in his own head.

'Yes, to protect the young mother and her child. The press would run stories because of Celine's death, and therefore the circumstances would have been front-page news. The family of the mother and daughter would have been hounded for months. Maybe years. He said it was felt that Celine would have wanted to protect them.'

Louis jerked his head up and down in what passed for a nod.

'She would never have wanted those families to go through any more pain than they would already have been in. Neither would she have wanted people pointing the finger at Rainbow House. Back then there were people who already objected to having a place for people with learning difficulties on their doorstep. My mother wouldn't want to have given them any more ammunition.'

'No one could never have anticipated that your father would use the cover-up to tell you such a cruel lie. You can't blame yourself.'

Fury howled inside him, tearing and clawing. He wanted to rage. At the world. At his parents. At himself.

'I don't,' he ground out.

And he didn't, at least not for that part of it. But how could he have believed his father—a man who made his career on lying and being vindictive as much as his talent—over what he knew in his heart to be true about his mother? How could he have ever imagined she would have chosen to take her own life? What kind of a son did that make him?

What kind of a person did that make him?

No loyalty. No trust. No belief.

Suddenly he realised Alex was cupping his face in her hands as though she could anchor him while the terrible storm wailed around his head. As though she could save him.

But she couldn't.

No one could.

He had to protect her. She deserved better, so much better, than him. She deserved someone loyal and honourable, someone who would stand by her side no matter what. Clearly, he wasn't that person. He never had been. The press were right.

'Tonight you will pack to leave. The wedding is off.'

'No,' she cried. 'That doesn't make sense.'

He'd only felt helpless once before in his life. The night his father had told him that his mother had given up on existence, on herself, on *him*, and taken her own life. Louis was determined that tonight, the night he had discovered it was all a lie, wasn't going to be a second time.

'It makes perfect sense.' He finally found the strength to move. To take Alex's hands and tear them away from his face. To step away from her. To cross the room. Seeing her desperation only made him feel furious, powerless and mournful all at once. He couldn't understand the emotions raging through him. He only knew that, whatever they were, they had to be as far removed from *love* as it was possible to get.

Because that was the one thing he clearly wasn't capable of.

'The only person at fault here is your father—you can't let him win. You must learn to forgive yourself.'

A tear tracked its way down her cheek and his stomach churned at the realisation that he'd hurt her. Immeasurably. He'd been a fool to imagine it could have turned out any other way.

But equally quickly, anger washed over the guilt. For her part, had Alex been honest with him? She certainly hadn't been honest with herself.

'Alex, we've been through this before. You talk

about me forgiving myself, but you still haven't forgiven yourself.'

Her eyes flashed, but he didn't miss the shadow of panic.

'Of course I have. That's why I volunteer at Rainbow House. Because I've accepted my past and I've made peace with it. I don't push it away like you do.'

'But you still haven't accepted it, Alex. You don't volunteer at Rainbow House because you're at peace with yourself, you volunteer because you're still trying to earn your father's love. You might have stopped blaming yourself for your mother's death, and for not being the saviour sibling you had been intended to be, but deep down you don't think your father has stopped blaming you.'

'That's enough,' Alex gasped, her hand pressed to her chest as if he was ripping out her very heart.

He knew he might as well have been.

But he couldn't stop now. He had to tell her, lay it all out there. She deserved better and he couldn't bear the thought of being the one to tie her down, trap her and disappoint her.

'You've spent decades trying to prove to him that you were worthy of being born. It's what's driven you to be a doctor, to volunteer at Rainbow House, to make a difference. It's why you're so determined to save me. You're trying to turn me into the son my mother wanted me to be because you can't turn your father into the dad you've needed him to be.'

'Stop!'

The strangled cry constricted his chest, tightening until he could barely breathe. It was nothing compared to Alex's ashen appearance. But she had to hear this, she had to understand what she was doing. And why.

'He loved your mother, he loved your brother and now he loves Rainbow House,' Louis said quietly. 'All the volunteering you do forces him to keep the door open to you, and appreciate your hard work. But I can't imagine how much it must eat away at you that he's never loved just *you*.'

'How could you be so cruel?' She shook her head, the words so quiet he had to strain to hear them.

'It may be cruel, but it's also the truth. You and I aren't so different. We have each buried our demons yet convinced ourselves we've dealt with them. If you stop thinking I'm deliberately trying to hurt you just long enough to think clearly, you would see that all the pushing you've been doing to get me to take on the Lefebvre Group is motivated by your need to go back to your father and tell him that Rainbow House is safe.'

'No.' She shook her head but the way she bit her lip betrayed her uncertainty.

'In your eyes, marrying me would be the ultimate sacrifice. The one thing that would prove to your father that you would do anything for him. But it won't work, Alex. He'll have Rainbow House but it won't be the magic cure you think it will be. It won't change the way he either does or doesn't love you.'

'You don't know that,' she managed hoarsely. It was all the admission that he needed.

Until that moment he hadn't realised how badly a tiny part of him wanted her to tell him that none of that mattered any more, that she loved him. The fact that she hadn't cut him deeper than he could have imagined possible.

'And then you'll just be left married to me. As miserable as my mother was with my father.'

'That's not true.'

He couldn't allow her tears to get to him. This was the best thing. For him and for Alex.

'It is true. And I won't do that to someone. Alex, I won't do that to *you*.'

He would find another way to save Rainbow House, whether it meant gaining control of the Lefebvre Group or not. But Alex would be free and he wouldn't be in her life to darken it.

She deserved better than that. Better than him.

He stalked across the room, the heavy walnut door bearing the full brunt of his frustration. And there, her face white and pinched, stood Brigitte, her hand raised to knock.

Shock bounced around the trio and then the older lady spoke, her voice as dignified as ever.

'Monsieur Étienne Morel is in the drawing room with his father Monsieur Alain Morel. They ask me to tell you that they have found a loophole. Something about there is no need for you and Mademoiselle Vardy to marry?'

'This proves nothing,' Jean-Baptiste sneered as he raised his head from the papers Louis had set on his desk barely a day later. 'I'm not signing a thing.'

'As you wish.' Louis dipped his head as though it didn't matter to him one way or another. 'Then the contract will go to the board instead.'

For perhaps the first time he realised that it *didn't* matter. He'd wasted so much time fire-fighting all the little blazes his father had always set in his path that he hadn't realised they'd sapped all his energy and stopped him from battling the infernos that he really wanted to tackle.

There were more important things than wasting time on Jean-Baptiste.

Like Alex.

Ever since last night he'd been replaying the argument in his head, wondering if he'd done the right thing, if he could have done things differently.

'You can't send it to the board. I won't authorise it,' his father ground out, desperately trying to appear in control.

Louis turned as if to leave, pausing only at the door.

'It isn't a matter of authorisation. There's a legal obligation for your board to see all documents that pertain to the Lefebvre Group. It will be dealt with by both teams of lawyers. I have no control over that.'

'I am Chairman of the Delaroche Foundation and I won't allow it,' Jean-Baptiste growled.

Rather like a child throwing a playground tantrum, Louis realised abruptly.

He shrugged and reached for the door handle.

'As I said, there is a legal obligation. Neither of us can interfere with that.'

'You're threatening me.'

'No.' Louis shook his head. 'I'm telling you the facts. I'm even offering you the opportunity to emerge with your reputation, not to mention your dignity, intact. Which, frankly, is more than you deserve.'

'You're blackmailing me into signing the Lefebvre Group over to you. You? Chairman? It's laughable.'

'No more laughable that letting you get away with snatching control of the group before my mother's body was even cold.' Louis didn't know how he restrained himself. 'And, for sake of clarity, I'll say again that I am not blackmailing you, I am presenting you with the facts.'

'If I sign the Lefebvre Group over to you then my reputation will be safe?' Jean-Baptiste's eyes glittered malevolently. 'You seem to forget that the Delaroche board is *my* board. I own them, every single one of them, and I'll destroy the Lefebvre Group before you even get there.'

'You can try, I suppose.' Louis felt unbreakable, totally in command, and he intended to hold onto that feeling for as long as he could. 'But I don't think you can. The Lefebvre Group is my mother's legacy, and you already tried to destroy it once before and failed. Now I owe it to her to keep it alive.'

'You think you owe anything to the woman who abandoned you?' Jean-Baptiste was almost incandescent. 'Do you forget that she took her own life rather than watch her only son, her only child, grow up? Is that what your little whore has taught you? To be weak and pathetic, and so desperate you'll pretend your mother didn't know what her choice would do to her kid?'

Not now. Not yet.

The madness that ravaged its way through him was destructive. Louis recognised that, and it was all he could not to let it cripple him at the knees. He bit back any response that might alert his father to the fact that he knew the truth. He needed those papers signed first.

'I'm claiming it, as she always wanted me to.'

'You're that desperate that you, of all people, are getting married. Do you think I didn't realise what it was all about, you making such a public spectacle of asking your nobody girlfriend to marry you?'

Something fired inside him. It was one thing for Jean-Baptiste to come after him, quite another to go after his sweet Alex. He wanted to lay his father out on the floor right now, but he couldn't afford to let his fury show.

'I asked Alex to marry me because I wanted to. Because I—' Shock hit him. He took a deep breath, the realisation washing over him. 'Because I love her.'

'You?' Jean-Baptise mocked. 'You don't know the first thing about love. You never had it, and, if your less than stellar history is anything to go by, you never gave it either.'

Because he hadn't thought he deserved it. Because he'd been ashamed that his mother hadn't loved him enough for it to stop her taking her own life. Because that's what his father had told him, and he'd stupidly believed everything Jean-Baptiste had said back then.

'Your mother never loved you enough. How could she? Look at you. But if she did, then maybe it was your inability to love her back that made her commit suicide.'

Louis steeled himself. But the pain never hit.

Not the way it once had.

Something inside him stood strong, true. Like a beacon of light. Something that Alex had put there.

'I love Alex,' Louis reiterated, barely recognising his own raw voice or the admission that he had tried to pretend wasn't true for far too long.

It was there, and it was real. He loved her. He wasn't sure when it had happened. Perhaps it had started from that first meeting, but now there was no denying it. No hiding.

'There is no wedding tomorrow, we called it off. We won't marry for you, or for a contract, or for Rainbow House. But one day we will marry. And it will be for love.'

'Beautiful sentiment.' The acidulous words were matched only by the unpleasant sneer and slow handclap. 'Though I'm not sure the press will buy it. Not when I tell them exactly what kind of sham your engagement has been.'

Louis stood, his palms flat on the table, his body leaning over, and took in the vicious gleam in his father's eyes as the old man waited for him to lose his temper.

Well, not today.

He could almost hear Alex's soft voice in his

head as he dredged up an icy smile, but a smile nonetheless. His voice was low and even.

'Fine. Go ahead and tell the media whatever you want. You're going to anyway. But don't pretend it's anything other than to destroy her reputation for your own revenge. And it won't change anything. You've still lost. I will take control of the Lefebvre Group and Rainbow House, which my mother and my grandfather worked so tirelessly to support. I don't need to marry Alex. I *want* to marry her.'

'I won't sign.'

'Then you'll end up losing the Delaroche Foundation, too,' Louis warned. Though, perhaps surprisingly, he took no pleasure from it. It was simply a fact that his stubborn father needed pointing out to him. 'If they see these papers—and they'll have to, there's no avoiding it—then you could lose everything.'

'No,' his father ground out, his composure beginning to crack. 'Take the Delaroche Foundation from me? I'd like to see you try.'

'I don't want your foundation,' Louis scorned. 'I never did. But I want to honour the legacy my mother created. The first seven years of my life were the happiest I've ever had, until now. She taught me how to laugh, how to be kind, and how to feel. I recognise now what I've always known, and that is that the only reason she would have chosen to leave me behind is if she hadn't been in her right mind. And that comes down to you. And you alone. We both know how cruelly you treated her.'

'You think you can blame her death on me? You dare to threaten me? *Pah,* the press will never believe a playboy bastard like you.'

He'd never seen his father's hand shake like that before.

Somehow it only helped Louis feel all the calmer.

'I wasn't threatening you at all.' He straightened up, making a show of taking a step back from the table. Away from his father. 'I have no intention of going to the media. I can't think of anything that's less their business. However, it will come out. The truth always does.'

'Then I'll destroy you,' Jean-Baptiste roared, his anger making him miss Louis's warning.

Wordlessly, Louis stood up straight and took a further step back from the desk. The moments ticked by as they remained motionless in their respective places. At an impasse. But Louis knew he held the key. He drew in a steadying breath, then another, and another. One image locked in his brain. Alex, in her wedding dress. And he knew with bone-deep certainty that he had to win her back. She was the one thing that made his life make sense. He could live without her if he had to, but he didn't want to have to.

'Sign the papers. It will return the group to me as my mother's will had always intended, and the fact that you manipulated the documents will never have to come out. Once the tie is severed between the Delaroche Foundation and the Lefebvre Group, all documents pertaining to the latter, including these, are no longer valid. As the new chairman of the Lefebvre Group, I can file them away wherever I see fit and neither your board, nor anyone else, need ever see them. It's your choice.'

'And yet it isn't really a choice at all, is it?' sneered the older man. Still, Louis found himself holding his breath as his father, with no other choice, lifted his pen and began to sign.

Personally, he would have liked nothing better than to let the whole world know what Jean-Baptiste had done, let him get his comeuppance. But that would destroy the Delaroche Foundation and there were too many good people, too many truly charitable projects that would be irreparably damaged by such an action. It would destroy far more than it would achieve.

And that wasn't something he could imagine Alex approving of. It was strange how much she factored into his thoughts. How, over their time together, he had begun to weigh things against what she might approve of or not.

He'd thought cutting her free was the right thing to do. The only thing to do. But now he wasn't so sure. She'd once told him she loved him. Had that been true? Could she love him again?

'There, you have your pound of flesh.' The resentful tone pulled Louis back to the moment.

He leaned over to take the papers but his father gripped them all the more tightly, one final insult at the ready.

'What would your mother think of you now?'

The insidiousness scratched at Louis, scraping away until a rage was rushing in to fill the vacuum. He twisted around and the sardonic smile on Jean-Baptiste's face revealed the old man thought he had won.

At any other time, he might have. But Louis had a weapon now, one he'd never had before—

Alex's belief in him. He knew it was pointless but he couldn't stop the glimmer of possibility that maybe, just maybe he could one day win her love for real.

He had to be the kind of man she deserved.

'I don't think you have the right to talk to me about my mother. Not now. Not ever.' He sounded as close to the edge as he felt. But that couldn't be helped.

The cruel twist of his father's mouth was sharp enough to draw blood. Like a scalpel slicing him from within.

Now.

'No wonder you weren't enough to make her want to live.'

It was all Louis could do to swallow the bitter, acid taste in his mouth.

'Except that she did want to live, didn't she? She never committed suicide, she never even considered it. The day she died she was trying to save a life, not take one. But you told me otherwise simply to keep me in line. To exact some kind of revenge.'

He'd never seen that expression on his father's face before. So hateful, so ugly.

'So you finally know the truth. How does it feel,

Louis, to know that you believed so badly of her so easily?'

'You're really trying to turn this onto me?'

'How much guilt do you feel, knowing that she believed in you so much that she bought a house a few streets away from Rainbow House, where she thought you and she could live, and yet you didn't believe in her enough to trust that she hadn't taken her own life?'

'She bought a house?' Louis echoed dully, as Jean-Baptiste's face contorted all the more.

'You must feel sick to the stomach to realise how pathetically easy it was to convince you that she had left you. You didn't have enough faith in her to question what I told you for even a moment.'

'You're sick.'

'I'm a winner. I do whatever it takes. And you're just like me. As this…' he waved his hand over the papers he'd just signed '…proves.'

He had a choice. He could let his father get to him, as he had always done. Or he could be the man Alex would want him to be, the man his mother would have wanted him to be, but, more importantly, the man *he* wanted to be.

And suddenly it was so clear. He was finally

free. Free from guilt and responsibility for things over which he actually had no control. Alex had freed him. Maybe she'd started to from the moment they had first met on that balcony, and now it was time he did the same for her.

And he knew just what he needed to do to win her back. If she'd let him, as he knew he'd really hurt her. But he had to try. Starting with resurrecting the plans for the stable block. Taking the papers from his father's hands and striding across to the door, Louis felt lighter and less weighed down than he had in years. Possibly ever.

'No,' he cast over his shoulder with a genuine smile that wasn't aimed at his father in the least. He felt jubilant, untethered, victorious. 'I'm nothing like you. I never have been.'

CHAPTER FOURTEEN

THE NEWS THAT Louis was back at Silveroaks reached Alex's ears at the end of a long afternoon of surgeries, her legs wobbling perilously as she checked on her last patient in the recovery unit. It had been three weeks, two days, seven hours and a handful of minutes since that awful row back at the chateau.

She knew the timings by heart. How could she not? The moment he'd walked out of that door it had been as though her life had been stripped of every last drop of colour. And now he was back.

But was it for work? Or for her?

She knew what was most likely, and yet hope still gurgled inside her like a trickling brook. The past few weeks had been like nothing she could describe—a deep, hollow emptiness that tumbled around her chest.

And as much as her heart ached for herself, it also ached for Louis. For what the two of them had almost shared. For how far he'd almost come.

For the way she'd hurt him without intending to. He'd hurt her too, she knew that, but it didn't stop her caring for him. She should have told him that he was becoming more important to her than Rainbow House, than her father. She knew what it was like, playing second best. Why had she made him feel as though he was?

It may not have changed anything, but at least she would have been brave enough to have been honest. For once. Because nothing eased the dull pain that still ached inside her every time she read a news story about a possible sighting of the uncharacteristically low-profile Louis, who still appeared to be working from the relatively secure confines of the chateau. Nothing, that was, until the news had filtered down that he was back.

And despite all attempts by her brain to caution her, it was as though that very fact in itself caused the colour to flow back into her lonely black and white world. And the voice in her head, which she'd been trying to silence for almost a month, finally broke free of its cage.

If you want him, go and find him.

She had no recollection of moving through the hospital, its maze of corridors which she knew so well, but one minute she was leaving the recovery unit and the next she was outside Louis's door. She lifted her hand to knock, then decided against it and simply stepped right in. This time her legs really did give way.

The room seemed to shrink around him, as though he overpowered it without doing a thing. Sitting behind the desk as he was, his shirtsleeves rolled up to reveal his tanned forearms, his tie loose and a stack of paperwork in front of him, how could he have grown more powerful, more handsome, more… *Louis* in a matter of weeks?

Stumbling back, she felt the door swing with her, heard it slam shut with such force the room shook.

Not exactly the entrance she'd been intending but at least he wouldn't know just how weak at the knees he made her.

He narrowed his eyes.

'Alex? What are you doing here?'

Her mouth had never felt so parched. She still couldn't find the strength to push off the door and so she stayed there, leaning against the cheap wood veneer, effectively trapping him.

'I came to see you.'

'Evidently.'

There was no trace of sarcasm in his tone and yet she could feel the heat rising from her toes.

'I came to apologise,' she said calmly. As if she wasn't shaking inside.

Even the frown that drew his features together was handsome. How had she forgotten quite how striking he was?

'I believe I should be the one apologising. I came here to tell you as much. I said things to you that were unforgivable.'

He'd been intending to see her? To talk to her? Something tiptoed through her but she didn't dare to examine it too closely. Not yet.

'You said things to me that were true.' Alex forced herself to maintain eye contact, but that familiar heat burned low in her. 'What's more, I needed to hear them. I know I've said this before, but you were right, I was just as tethered to my past as you. I was using you, our marriage, to try to convince my father that I would do anything for him. To try to make him love me the way he loved my brother.'

Was that sadness that skittered across his expression before he shut it down? She couldn't quite tell. He leaned back in his chair, his eyes raking over her even though his voice was gentle.

'Did it turn out the way you hoped?'

'No. But it turned out exactly the way you said it would.' And somehow, with Louis, it didn't hurt as much as it had. 'My father was pleased, perhaps grateful, but he didn't have some epiphany. He didn't suddenly tell me how much he loved me, or how proud of me he was. And I realised that he never would.'

'I'm sorry.'

She blinked back the tears that pricked her eyes.

'I realise that he never will. He loves me in his own way, but it will never be the limitless, unconditional way he loved Jack or my mother. I'll never know what he really feels about me, and whether deep down a part of him blames me or not, but I do know that I don't blame myself. I live my life as well as I can and if that's enough for him then great. If not, I refuse to twist myself inside out for him any longer. I'm me, and I'm happy with who I am.'

'That's good.' Louis smiled softly and it tugged at her chest, her stomach, lower.

'And I have you to thank for helping me to see that.'

Finally, finally, she found the strength to push

off from the door, to make it halfway across the room before she stopped.

'You gave me the strength to trust in myself. You've allowed me to believe in myself,' she murmured. 'But you were wrong about one thing.'

He was watchful, immobile.

'And what was that?'

'I may not have recognised my underlying intentions, but I was genuine when I told you I wanted to help you stop punishing yourself. I thought I could help you move on.'

The silence stretched out between them. For a moment she thought he wasn't going to answer.

'You did help me,' he said abruptly. 'Because of you I realised I no longer felt the isolation I'd never realised I'd been experiencing. My brain was fired up with a renewed drive. I had this… this energy effervescing in my blood. Alex, you made me feel *alive*.'

The hot—even savage—need in his eyes was almost her undoing.

He didn't remember reaching into his drawer, or standing up to cross the room and stand in front of her, the pretty leather box offered to her with as much ceremony as if it were a ring.

Her arrival had been as unexpected as it had been incredible, filling him with feelings he hadn't dared to let himself experience these last few weeks. Pouring hope and light right through him. He fought the urge to scoop her into his arms and hold her close to him to try to make her feel safe, secure, cared for—to make *him* feel all those things—and simply waited for her to open the box.

'A key?'

Her surprise was evident and, despite himself, laughter spilled from his lips. *His* Alex. If she would let him.

'Not just any key. It's the key to Rainbow Court Respite Holidays in what was once the stable block of Chateau Rochepont.'

'Rainbow Court Respite Holidays?' She turned the words over and over on her tongue as though she couldn't quite believe it.

'It was what my mother had always intended to do with the place,' he said softly. 'It's what you kept pushing me to do. I told you I'd consider it.'

'I remember.' She flushed. 'But I was pushing for all the wrong reasons. I should never have done that to you. It doesn't matter any more. I don't need it. I just need you.'

'And I didn't do this for you.' He pulled a wry face. 'Well, not entirely. I did it for myself. Because seeing her legacy come to fruition was something I needed to do for me. I made it one of the first things I did as the chairman of the new board of the Lefebvre Group.'

She blinked at him, then back down to the key.

'I thought you would sell the group after all.'

'Someone convinced me to change my mind. Someone whose opinion I respect. Someone who… I love.'

'Love,' the word was echoed with such awe that it scraped and teased across every inch of his body. It felt more right than he could have ever imagined to take her hands and repeat his vow to her.

'I love you, Alexandra. You enrich my life and make me want to be a better man than I ever dreamed I could be. Marry me. Not for Rainbow House, or for the Lefebvre Group, but simply to be my wife. To spend the rest of our lives making each other happy.'

And when she kissed him, the certainty in her eyes shining out brighter than any jewel that could ever exist, any last shadows of the demons that had lurked inside both of them were finally banished for good.

'Say the words,' he commanded, finding himself wanting to hear them. Needing her to voice them.

'Which words?' she murmured against his mouth, hot and inviting and sensual. Teasing him as though they had all the time in the world. And maybe they did. 'Oh, you mean tell you I love you?'

'I warn you.' He bit gently at her lip as she squirmed in pleasure. 'Two can play that game.'

'I'm counting on it.' She rocked against him, deliberately slowly, provocatively. 'Which is exactly *why* I love you.'

'Again.'

'I love you, Louis.'

And he knew, with bone-deep conviction, that his redemption was complete. Alex was his just as he would always be hers. Not because there was a means to an end but because this *was* the end. And the beginning.

This time was for real.

* * * * *